'As we came out of the forest near Euny's hut, and I
saw the great shadow of the tor above us I felt a little
shiver of excitement and joy. It was not dark, but
already a brilliant sliver of a moon hung in the sky
over the tor. Rain had made a pool on the grass in front
of the hill and sitting upon it were twelve swans, their
beautiful heads and wings mirrored in the water. The
sun shone upon the tor at an angle that lit it strangely.
Its bare, terraced sides were shadowed, its outline
haloed. Euny and I stood quite still and Euny made
some exclamation under her breath – it might have
been an incantation or a prayer.

I saw the moon through the branches of the hazel tree,
and the outline of the hill springing behind it, and I
knew that this was the place where I should be . . . '

Ninnoc, a pampered Cornish princess, is horrified when
she learns that she must go to stay with her godmother
Euny, a shabby and bad-tempered woman who lives in
the Outlands. But Euny is a wise woman, and there are
things that only she can teach Ninnoc . . .

An exciting and memorable fantasy, *Juniper* is Monica
Furlong's second title to be published by Corgi Books.
Already available is *Wise Child*, a sequel to *Juniper*.

d published by Corgi Books:

MONICA FU

ISE CHILD

JUNI

CORGI BO

Contents

Chapter One

A Remarkable Child

The night I was born, according to my nurse Erith, was a night of black frost and dense darkness in a bitter January. What gave a particular strangeness to it was that the white owls who lived in some nearby trees never stopped hooting and flying around the palace all night. No-one slept a wink. Erith thought that it was a sign that I was a very remarkable child, and, by the time I was old enough to hear the story, I liked to believe her. Remarkable or not, I was bathed and oiled and bandaged as all babies are and then they dressed me in a little shift and wrapped me in a rabbit skin to keep me warm. My mother and father showed their first baby to the ealdors, the elder statesmen, as was the custom, and then Erith cuddled me all night so that, as she said, I would not feel strange in this new country I had come to. In fact, I grew and flourished in it, loved by my mother Erlain, my father Mark, and Erith my nurse.

My father was *regulus,* that is a small chieftain or king, in Cornwall, and we lived at Castle Dore, in the Wooden Palace that he had built on a high grassy place – the site of an ancient fort. There was a house round a courtyard where my mother and father and I lived, a house for the astrologers and another for the bards, an armoury, a bakery, quarters for the knights and ealdors, and a big hall where my father dined with them every evening. The house was high in the hills with a long view of farms and other hills, and the air sparkled with that special radiance of Cornish light.

My mother Erlain was a tall, graceful woman who was very clever. She could read and write, and had learned mathematics and poetry. She could sing beautifully to the harp, and it was she, I heard tell, who brought the bards to our house and, with them, a very different atmosphere from the days when my father had lived alone with his knights. She taught him to read and write and gradually, warrior that he was, he began to enjoy learning as much as she did. Later on, as a result of that, he wanted me to have the sort of good education that girls often do not have even now.

But I go too fast. I should tell you that whenever a child was born to a knight or ealdor among my people the astrologers studied the heavens, and its charts, to work out the portents for its life. Then they wrote some words, almost a sort of poem, to help the child remember the main points and this was inscribed in tiny writing on parchment and put in a little horn case which you wore on a leather thong round your neck. Later on, when I was older and had learned to read, I liked to take the parchment out and read the words through, just to remind myself. They went like this:

Named for the strong and twisting tree
Of medicine, when she finds the way
By earth, air, water, fire

Then will she mend what is broken.
The dark teacher will correct her
The fair one will protect her
The strong man will love her
And all may be well.

It didn't make much sense to me because after all, I was *not* named after a tree, but was called by the good Cornish name of Ninnoc. The rest of the words seemed just as puzzling.

My earliest memories are of a huge chamber at the Wooden Palace with a fire leaping and flickering in the hearth. I had a big bed and Erith had a little one in the corner, but because I felt lonely in my big bed I often jumped out of it and climbed in with Erith. Erith was young and pretty, with red hair and lots of freckles. I used to count them to tease her. Sometimes I woke her to make her tell me a story or sing me one of her Irish songs. I was quite bossy with Erith – I behaved like a little princess who expects the servants to do as she tells them – refusing to get dressed or have a bath or eat my dinner or whatever it was she had to get me to do. Once or twice she threatened to tell my father about my bad behaviour, but she never did.

Sometimes my father appeared in my apartment in the evening just at the time I should be going to bed, and told Erith to dress me in my prettiest gown. (I had some beautiful clothes made from pieces of gold or silver material like liquid flame left over from my mother's gowns. I was very proud of myself in them.) I had earrings and bracelets made of silver or set with gems, and on special occasions Erith hung jewels in my long black hair. So Erith would put on my little squirrel-skin slippers, and comb my hair, and then I would walk with my father in the procession to the Great Hall. He would sit me on his lap, feed me titbits from his plate, and after dinner I would be passed around the knees of the knights and they all teased me and played with me. Once or twice I stood up on the table and sang one of the songs my mother or Erith had taught me.

I was disappointed that my mother did not have another baby who could have been a playmate for me. Only much later did I realize that my parents also wanted more children. But soon I acquired a new playmate whom I will tell you about later and in addition Erith let me play with the children of some of the knights and ealdors. We played marvellous games. The old fort on which the palace was built had been surrounded by enormous ditches and ramparts built in a maze to make it hard for an enemy to find the way in. We raced each other round the ditches, slid down the ramparts on wooden sleds, learned the mazes by heart and had wonderful games of hide-and-seek there.

Once, when we were playing, a thin, dark-skinned woman approached the entrance to the maze which led to the palace. She had strange black eyes, high colour in her cheeks, and a strong, determined gait. She was dressed in worn black clothes, not much better than rags really, and she wore no head covering as all the grown women did except the beggars. Her black hair, instead of being dressed, hung straight down her back, as if she was a child. She wore boots so old that part of her foot showed through most of one of them. Her whole appearance offended me.

'What do you want here?' I asked bossily.

'I have business with Marcus Cunomorus,' she said, sweeping me aside and moving into the maze.

'He won't see you!' I shouted scornfully to her back. After which we children climbed up on to the ramparts for the pleasure of seeing her lose her way in the maze. (We had often enjoyed seeing strangers turn repeatedly up the blind alleys until they were forced to ask our help and even to bribe us with a coin.) The thin woman did not lose her way but moved skilfully towards the entrance, and the guard must have let her through because a few minutes later we could see her making her way towards my father's apartments.

'Who was that woman who came to see you?' I asked him that evening. 'The one in dreadful clothes.'

'That was Euny,' he said, and was silent, though he and my mother exchanged glances. I wanted to ask who she was and what she had come for, but he discouraged me always from asking about things that were not my business, so that I did not quite dare. I was always a little afraid of him.

I have a much earlier memory that I somehow associate with meeting Euny, as if it gave me a hint of events to come. I was quite small, was toddling round on the big grassy enclosure at the centre of the fort. Many grown-ups were walking about, men mostly, holding strange forked twigs in their hands. They moved slowly, eyes fixed on the ground, and they did not notice me or talk to me as they usually did. Because I was bored, and wanted to copy them, I picked up one of the forked twigs that someone had dropped, and began to move towards the middle of the grass. Suddenly I screamed and screamed, so wildly and in such terror that everyone stopped and looked at me. What had happened was that the twig in my hand had turned into a snake. Well, it hadn't really. It was just an old twig, but while I had held it, all of a sudden it had started moving and wriggling in my hand in the most horrible way. My father came over to me.

'What happened?' he asked.

'It turned into a snake,' I said, knowing that they would all laugh at me because there it was just being a stick.

'It's all right,' he said. 'It wasn't really a snake. Would you do it again to show us?'

So, rather nervously, but wanting to please, I picked up the twig again by its two handles, and almost at once it began to jerk upwards as if it had a life of its own, and once again I dropped it with a yell. I thought my father would be cross with me, but he picked me up in his arms with a laugh.

'Well done, little girl. You've found us another supply of water. We thought there was one here somewhere but no-one could ever find it.'

It was soon after this that I found a tiny baby owl out in the fields and since he appeared to have lost his mother and to be in a sad, bedraggled condition, I insisted on taking him home. Erith kept saying that my parents would not allow me to keep him, but I hid him in a small room off my sleeping chamber and only she ever knew. Erith was sure that I would not bother to feed him, but I used to beg mice that the cook had caught in her traps, and other little pieces of meat, and the baby owl seemed quite content. His feathers looked clean now, especially when he fluffed himself out. I loved to take him upon my hand and stare into his blank amber eyes. Sometimes he sat upon my shoulder, but often he liked to perch for hours on a shelf over the hearth, dozing in the dim winter light. Later he took little flights about the room, moving beautifully upon his wide wings. I called him Moon.

As I grew older I am sorry to say that I became ruder to Erith. She was often quite worn-out with the effort of getting me to get up, wash and dress, even though it was she who did the work of washing and dressing me. I could never do anything to look after myself in those days. When we went out I was always wanting to go further than was permitted, or to do things which Erith thought were dangerous – walking on the ice of ponds when it was still too thin, jumping over the autumn bonfires that the farm people built at harvest time, climbing high into trees, swinging from one branch to another and refusing to come down. Erith would stand imploring me to do as I was told, torn between her love and care for me and her fear of heights or of water or of fire. In those days I seemed to be afraid of nothing.

I was tormenting Erith like this one day. I had gone into the stable where my father's stallion was kept, a great black animal who had lamed a groom and whose kick could probably have killed me. I moved nearer and nearer to it, determined to stroke it and give it an apple, while Erith, half-crying, beseeched me to return to her. I think I knew that I was being very silly, but somehow Erith's pleas drove me on to misbehave.

Suddenly, to my amazement, I felt myself seized by my neck and shoulders and marched out of the stable by someone behind me whom I could not see. As soon as they dropped their hold I turned furiously round and was astonished to see that it was the woman Euny, still as shabby as ever, gazing at me with blazing eyes.

'Juniper!' she said. We stood and stared at each other for a few moments, both of us angry, and then, annoyed that she was rebuking me for distressing Erith, I mumbled, 'It's not your business, anyway.'

Euny did not reply to this but gave me a little push in the direction away from the stable and herself turned and walked off. Glancing at Erith I saw that she looked sickeningly smug.

'There!' she said. 'You've annoyed your godmother.'

I was so surprised at this that I forgot about her looking smug.

'My godmother! Euny my godmother! Why would someone like Euny be my godmother?'

'That was your mother's choice,' she said. 'Not that your father disagreed.' And she closed her lips very firmly in a way she had when I talked about things that made her uneasy.

So naturally I asked my mother Erlain at the first opportunity.

'Is Euny my godmother?'

'Yes.'

'Why?'

'Because she is wise. And we needed her.'

'Why?'

'I can't tell you now.'

14

'I don't like her. She looks like a beggar woman.'
My mother did not answer.

'And she called me Juniper. Why was that?'
My mother laughed with pleasure.

'It was a special name she had for you, your secret name. She whispered it in your ear when you were a baby. Later she told me and said that the secret name was who you really are.'

All this seemed very peculiar to me, though not so peculiar as the fact that my parents had asked this strange woman to be my godmother in the first place. I went out and walked in the ditch between the ramparts to think – a place I often walked when I wanted peace and quiet. There, between the grassy walls and under a grey spring sky, I tried out the name for sound and meaning.

'Juniper. Juniper. Juniper!'

As I spoke it an extraordinary sense of conviction seized me, as if I had moved and saw the world more clearly and freshly from this new place.

'Juniper!' I said it more loudly, and finally I shouted it as hard as I could.

A sentry's face looked reproachfully over the top of the ramparts.

'Now then!' he said kindly, meaning that making loud noises was worrying to a man whose job was to look out for sudden attacks by our enemies. But I had finished. I knew that Euny, however odd, was right, and that Juniper was my proper name. Later on I had another question for my mother.

'Where does Euny live?'

'She's an Outlander.' That meant that she lived in the country out beyond the farms that were under my father's special protection, in a place where she was always in danger of marauders and brigands.

'Doesn't that frighten her?'

'Not Euny. I don't believe she's ever afraid.'

Chapter Two

Gamal

There was only one person at the court whom I disliked, and whom I felt disliked me in return – my aunt Meroot. She was my father's older sister. All his life he had loved and admired her, so that when I said that I did not like her he would tell me sharply not to be silly. When I was about four Meroot's husband died in mysterious circumstances. My father had a house built for her in the Wooden Palace and she came to live with us with her son Gamal who was about my age. Unlike my father, who had wonderful ruddy hair and powerful blue eyes, Meroot had sandy hair, and eyes like cold, pale sapphires, that I felt watched me critically from behind the curtain of her white lashes. Gamal, on the other hand, was a handsome, blond-haired little boy, not at all like his mother. At once he became a brother to me – we played, slept, ate together a lot of the time – but so far as we possibly could we kept out of Meroot's way. Meroot, whom my father used jokingly to say would have made a wonderful soldier, was determined that Gamal should grow up strong and fearless, and almost from when he was a baby she had little suits of armour and small swords made for him, and had him trained in fighting and wrestling and archery at an age when most little boys were playing marbles or looking for birds' eggs. She made him wear very few clothes in the winter so that he would become tough (it had the effect of giving him endless colds), she forced him to sleep on the hard floor with few blankets and to eat the sort of diet soldiers ate. It was a hard life.

Gamal was very loyal to his mother and hardly ever complained, but as a result of these hardships he spent a lot of time getting warm at the fire in my apartment, wearing a rough coat Erith stitched for him out of a blanket, eating any spare food we had, and occasionally dozing off to sleep in corners. In spite of his mother's treatment he was a cheerful, uncomplaining boy, who worked hard at all the strenuous training Meroot prepared for him, but secretly learned to read. He was very musical – a gift Meroot thought wasted on a future soldier. It was lucky she did not know the hours he spent in our house playing any instrument he could lay his hands on. He composed tunes, too, and put words to them. There was one very special song he used to sing, a lullaby, the rhythm of which haunts me still.

'Where did you learn that?' I asked him. A slightly puzzled look came over his face.

'A woman taught it to me,' he said. 'A woman with fair hair like mine.'

'Was she your nurse?'

Gamal hesitated. 'I don't know,' he said.

I knew by his air of embarrassment that there was something mysterious about the song that he himself could not explain.

Even apart from her treatment of Gamal I never liked Meroot. She always *seemed* to be kind to me, drawing me to her and kissing me, stroking my hair, using flattering words, bringing me presents from her frequent travels, but there was something about her that made me uneasy. Her words sounded false, and I felt that although she claimed to love me, actually she didn't really like me at all. Once, when Gamal and I, aged about five, were alone with her in her apartment we were having a quarrel over a toy, a wooden bird with moving wings. We shouted at one another and grabbed the bird backwards and forwards between us. Suddenly Meroot, her eyes blazing, leaned over, smacked me, snatched the toy from my grasp and gave it to Gamal. The look that she gave me was one of pure hatred, and I shrank back from her. I never trusted her after that.

Soon I realized that my mother's lips tightened whenever Meroot's name was mentioned and that she never entertained her except on official occasions when her absence would have been noticed. Once when Aunt Meroot was away on one of her journeys and Gamal was happily living in our house I said to my mother, 'Wouldn't it be nice if Aunt Meroot never came back?' My mother laughed in a slightly rebuking way, as grown-ups do when they agree with you, but don't want you to know it, but I could see that she felt just as I did, and that, like me and Erith, she enjoyed spoiling Gamal as if to counteract Meroot's influence.

I spent a lot of time with my mother just then. Usually she was a woman who liked her own company and she would sit contentedly for hours in her apartment, reading or sewing. Yet when I wandered in from playing or riding my pony she seemed pleased to see me and we had long conversations together.

In one of these I was surprised to discover that Meroot, just like Euny, had been my godmother. I tried to get Erlain to discuss it, but she would say nothing except, 'She is your father's sister.' But her face was cold and her lips disapproving and I guessed that the choice had not pleased her.

'Why is Meroot so nasty to Gamal?' I asked. 'She makes him sleep in that cold room without proper blankets.'

'She wants to make him a great warrior,' she replied. 'Don't fiddle with that cup, dear. You may drop it.'

'I can't be a great warrior,' I said.

'No,' she said, her eyes meeting mine, 'you will need other powers.'

'What other powers?'

'It is too soon to say.'

'If I had a brother would he rule the kingdom after father?'

'Yes,' said my mother, expressionless.

'But if I don't have a brother?'

'That would depend,' she said. 'On your power. The strength of the warrior is not the only kind.'

I went out to the ditch to think things out, and, crouching up against the grassy rampart, I wondered whether I had any power. I didn't feel as if I did, although I *had* used special powers to find water. I had not set out to use them, however. It had simply happened when I wasn't thinking about it. I couldn't see that that would be much use in running a kingdom and I could well imagine that, if my mother did not bear a son, a powerful knight or a distant cousin might take the kingdom over or . . . Gamal . . .!

Just as his name occurred to me a pebble struck me lightly on the head, there was a shout from up

20

above and Gamal slithered down the bank beside me and landed with a bump at the bottom. It was as if thinking about him had brought him there.

'Gamal!'

'Mother's away and I've got the afternoon free from swordplay. Let's go somewhere.'

The two of us saddled our horses and rode away, galloping over the moorland towards the distant sea. We made for a little valley, quite deserted, where the horses moved down tracks between the trees towards a stream that led to the sea. When we reached the sandy beach we threw off our clothes and plunged into the waves. Afterwards, sunning ourselves on the rocks, we played a game of seeing how long we could sit on one rock before the incoming tide engulfed us. We had the sense to know that if we waited too long it would be really dangerous, but it was fascinating to see how long the sea took, making occasional bold sallies further up the beach, and then, as if preparing to trick us, not moving in our direction for a long, long time.

'Will *you* become *regulus* of Cornwall when my father dies?' I asked Gamal bluntly. 'Is that what Meroot wants?'

Gamal reddened. 'It's what she wants. It doesn't mean it will happen.' Then he added, 'Your mother may have a son.'

'And if she doesn't?'

Gamal shrugged. I considered for a bit, and then remembered my mother's words.

'The strength of the warrior is not the only kind of strength,' I repeated. 'There are other kinds of power. I intend to learn what they are, and, as my father's daughter, to rule after him.'

Gamal gave me a long, thoughtful glance.

'I hope you do,' he said. 'As you know, I want to be a musician, not a ruler, though mother would never let me.' He stood up as if the game with the tide no longer interested him. 'If you have the power to rule and do it rightly you will have my allegiance and my fealty,' he said. 'I would be glad to serve you.' He pretended to take the cap off his head (he wasn't wearing one, of course), and he swept a low bow to me. Then he climbed on his horse and rode away.

I was surprised and touched by his response, by the love and faithfulness in his grey eyes, and by the fact that he had not mocked my claims to power. But I suddenly felt very weak and frightened.

It was around that period that I began to dream – a dream that always had the same ingredients, except that each time the action proceeded a little further, and each time I woke up with a worrying sense that there was something I should do about the dream, only I could not imagine what it was. This feeling was slight at first but grew stronger and stronger.

The first part of the dream was tranquil and beautiful. There was a hazel tree with a full moon hanging in the sky beyond it which lit its leaves and branches until they shone like jewels. This passed into a sense of flying in a night sky rich with stars. Up to this point the dream was delightful, but then suddenly I was in a dark tunnel. I was not alone – I was running, terror-stricken, with some other people, and there was a deafening sound in our ears that I could not identify – was it thunder? As if the sound and the noise were not bad enough there was a most peculiar smell, as of a wild beast, which inspired a sense of fear. I discussed this dream, at my mother's suggestion, with one of the astrologers attached to the court, but though my people thought dreams were very important, he seemed unwilling to ponder what it might mean. I think he was afraid that he might have to prophesy a terrible accident, or even worse, and he preferred not to think about it. So, I struggled to think about it all by myself, but, apart from remembering that hazel was the wood we had used to find water, on the day the twig turned into a snake, I could make nothing of it.

As I grew older I spent less time with Erith and more with my tutors and my mother. I liked learning, most of the time, and I had the best of teachers. I had long outstripped Gamal, who spent most of his day in mock battles on the green enclosure where the men shot and wrestled and practised with their weapons. Only in music, even though his fingers were tired and wrenched from his day's exercise, could he outshine me. He played beautifully upon harp and flute, and he could sing well too, in a pure angelic treble. Most afternoons, sweaty, tired, hungry, he would come to see me after a day of wrestling or riding or sword-play. I too had finished my day's work – writing, translating, listening to my father giving judgement on a difficult case. Erith would bring both of us scented water in which to wash, and we would change our clothes. Then we ate some fruit or sweetmeats and settled down to play. Even Meroot did not forbid this. On wet days we played chess, or we made music. On fine days we walked or rode, coming home in the twilight to share a stew or roasted bird in front of the fire.

Together, too, we played with Moon, who liked to walk up our arms and sit on our shoulders. He had a way of apparently listening to our conversations, his head on one side, a thoughtful, judicial expression on his face that was irresistibly funny. Gamal often addressed questions to him, then replied in a pretend owl voice.

'Isn't Ninnoc in a bad temper today, Moon?' Gamal would ask and then reply owlishly to himself, 'I don't know what you're complaining about. I have to put up with her all the time.'

Gamal and I had begun to share a secret. When, day by day, he returned from his labours as an apprentice soldier, he was often cut or bruised. He would have a long scratch down his face, a nasty graze on his leg, a pulled shoulder, a twisted ankle. To begin with I would bathe these injuries for him, put ointment on them, bandage them, until we began to notice something strange. The injuries began to grow better as soon as I looked at them, or touched them, and often before I had reached for the bandage.

'Don't tell anyone!' I begged him, suddenly shy at this discovery.

'What is it that you do?' he asked me. That was the embarrassing part. I didn't *do* anything, just looked at the sore place and touched it and did whatever was necessary to make it feel better.

'I wonder what you *couldn't* heal?' Gamal went on. A week later we had the chance to find out. He came in with his arm broken after a bout of wrestling in which he had slipped and fallen. His tutor stood at the door waiting to take him to the bone-setter but Gamal insisted on coming to

24

me first. Seeing his face twisted with pain, and the protective way he held his arm, I put out a hand and touched him with the utmost gentleness. This time, because it was so important to make him better, I concentrated really hard on the thought of his broken arm. Nothing happened. We had discovered the limit of my power. I could manage cuts, scratches and bruises, but anything else was beyond me.

Chapter Three

The Hazel Tree

Since the day when she had found me in the stable Euny had not spoken to me again, which I thought was odd behaviour for a godmother. Perhaps twice a year I would see her at Castle Dore, marching purposefully through the palace on her way to my father's apartments. I noticed that once there she spent hours with him, but then, scorning the feasting and presents with which we regaled most of our visitors, she would leave as simply as she came, setting off on the long walk to the mysterious place where she lived in the Outland. I had no idea what she and my father could talk about.

One day, however, a change came. Erith entered the room where I was practising my calligraphy – I remember that I was gilding a letter A that had a tiny blue man sitting sideways on the cross bar and swinging his leg – and said, 'King Mark wants to see you. Right away.' She turned sharply and went out. I sighed – I had been enjoying my work and was annoyed at being interrupted, but no-one kept my father waiting. I suppose because that day changed my life I can still remember the look of the writing, the brilliant autumn day, and even the gown I wore – blue, with a belt worked in precious stones and silk.

My father sat in the great chair that he used when he was meeting people officially and on a smaller chair beside him, very upright, sat Euny, who did not greet or notice me. I sat on an even smaller chair, suddenly feeling insignificant and shy.

'We have been talking,' said my father, 'Euny and I, about your future. As you know, it is the custom of this country to send a noble child away from home for a year or two, to stay in another house as part of that child's education. It is usually boys who are sent, but in this case the circumstances are unusual. Euny, as your godmother, has proposed that in, say, a year's time, we should send you to live with her for a while. She believes, and I agree with her, that she will have valuable lessons to teach you.'

The expression on my face must have betrayed my horror at the idea of living with Euny, because my father frowned sternly at me. I had forgotten that, however startled I was, he expected me to show good manners.

'Go away from here!' I said. 'From Erith and you and Mother and Gamal and everyone? To go and live *in the Outland?*'

'You will come to no harm.'

I was so upset that I felt my lower lip begin to droop with the threat of tears. Euny spoke, but she was not in the least reassuring.

'It is necessary,' she said. 'There are things you need to learn — I have always noticed that you are spoilt here — things which only I can teach you. I am your godmother and I claim the right to instruct you.'

'I don't want to go,' I said sullenly, half under my breath.

'For a year and a day,' Euny went on as if I had not spoken. 'That should do it. You will come to me in about a year. I shall not send for you — you will know when the moment comes. Come alone, on foot, with a few clothes — that should suffice.'

'Very well, then,' said my father. 'It's settled.' I knew that this was the signal for me to leave, and unwillingly I got up to go. Euny followed me, and when we were outside the door, she turned to me with a rather wolfish smile, hissing through her teeth the one word, 'Juniper!' almost as if she was making a joke. Then she turned and walked away.

I was deeply shaken by this encounter. I discussed it with Erith, who was indignant at the suggestion that I should go anywhere without her, and I mentioned it to my mother, Erlain, who was sympathetic but who, predictably, sided with my father. However, she shed a new light on the idea.

'You have spoken of the power you may need one day,' she said. 'I think it is too soon to say whether you will have that, or should use it, but Euny is one who has power. That was why we chose her for you as a godmother. She is quite right — you could learn from her.'

This made the whole idea seem a little better, but at the same time I dreaded leaving all the places and people that I knew and going to live in the Outland.

'What is Euny's house like?' I asked sulkily.

'I don't know. I have never been there. I've heard that it is beside a great hill — a tor — near the sea, and I think she appoints herself a sort of guardian of the hill.'

This was comforting in a way – I liked the idea of living by the sea – but I was still puzzled. And hurt.

'You will send me to the Outland to stay at a house you have never seen? The Outland is *dangerous* – everybody knows that. I might easily be killed by brigands, or by our enemies. None of you seems to care. And Euny is so dirty and horrible.'

Quite apart from the dangers of the Outland I could not understand why my parents trusted Euny so much. I did not like Euny, nor trust her, and I was afraid of her rags and poverty.

My mother hesitated.

'The Christians say that there is no magic – that the world is ruled by love. I cannot decide whether they are right. Our forebear Arthur was a Christian yet believed in magic,' she said. '*This* kingdom seems to be controlled by magic, good magic and bad magic. For those who choose the good magic it is important to have strong allies who choose good magic too. Euny is your father's strongest ally – while she is his friend the bad magic will never overwhelm our kingdom. If you let her she will become your ally, and that may be important.'

Erlain said all this very gravely, and though the words she used were simple, it was as if she was talking to a grown-up. Somehow, without really understanding, I knew that I would have to go to be Euny's pupil.

I wondered when. Euny had said in about a year and that I would know when the time came, but I could not imagine how. In any case, a year seemed a comfortably long time away.

For a while after talking to Erlain I forgot about my assignment with Euny, or, when it did come into my mind, I would think perhaps that it would never really happen.

Autumn slipped into a snowy winter, and little seemed to have changed in my life. Except one thing. The dream of the hazel tree was coming more and more often. Always I was delighted by its beauty – it filled me with a sort of hunger that was also a kind of joy, the feeling that if I could find it I should be supremely happy. Occasionally I woke up at this point and there were tears of happiness on my cheeks. But far more often I was back again in the tunnel, running in terror from the dreadful fate which pursued me and my companions, and which was heralded by the intolerable noise and smell.

I told Gamal about the conversation with Euny. He was so fascinated that he went right home and told Meroot, and he later said that she was 'very angry' about it. I could not understand why it should make Meroot angry, but I was not in the least sorry that it did so.

I grew a lot in that year and felt as if I came to understand many more things. I played the harp every day, I learned and sang many of the famous songs of my people, I studied the stars and learned astrological law, I read Latin and wrote what I believed was a beautiful script. More often my father took me into his council chamber when he was listening to a dispute and afterwards he would ask me what I thought of his decision. I usually got bored in the middle of all the explanations, though, and went off into a day-dream. I day-dreamed a lot at that time. Sometimes I day-dreamed that I was a beautiful woman whom everybody adored, sometimes that I was a brave soldier who was afraid of nothing.

One day something odd happened, as odd as the day when I had felt the twig move in my hands. It was a bright spring morning and Gamal and I had run away, in my case from lessons and in Gamal's from the perpetual wearisome drilling of his life as a boy-soldier. We were riding, a long way from Castle Dore, in the Outland territory that my father had forbidden to us. We were cantering in a wide grassy space with trees on one side of it. I knew from previous experience that, a bit further on, the ground rose steeply, passed into a narrow gully by a stream with cliffs on both sides, swung towards a narrow place where you could only pass one at a time, and then opened towards an estuary and the sea.

I suppose I was thinking about the place, anticipating it, when suddenly, with total clarity I saw it in my mind's eye. On the far side of the narrow gorge was a camp with ragged women and children and skinny horses grazing. But in the narrow place between the rocks several men were crouched holding weapons, clearly with the intention of killing or holding to ransom any-one who attempted to pass. So vivid was this picture that I had to look around me to make sure that I was not actually at the gorge. No, there was the spacious stretch of grass, the trees, and the lithe movement of our horses beneath us. But there we were, it seemed to me, heading fast towards danger.

At once I told myself I was making up a story and that I must order my thoughts, but then, as if from beside me, came a voice, very like the owlish

voice in which Gamal imitated Moon, 'Don't go
. . . don't go.' On that day, as on many others, I
was carrying Moon asleep in my pocket. I slowed
my horse and although I knew the owl hated
bright daylight I pulled him out. He fluffed his
feathers, blinked crossly, and said again (I could
see his beak moving), 'Don't go . . . don't go.'

'You can talk, Moon!' I said.

'Of course,' he replied wearily. 'But now I want
to go back to sleep.'

I shouted to Gamal to stop, reined in my own
horse, and slipped to the ground. He rode back
to me, puzzled. He was even more puzzled when
I told him.

'You just made that up!' he said.

'Perhaps I did. I'm not sure. But I am quite
certain that if we ride through the gorge we will
be in danger.'

Gamal chewed thoughtfully on a piece of grass.

'In that case, how about climbing that path up
above the gorge – you remember the one – and
looking down on the camp? Just to see.'

I did not want to appear a coward, so I swallowed my longing to turn and go home and
set off with him on foot along a path through
the trees. There was something very reassuring
about having an adventure with Gamal. He had
such a sensible, cheerful air as he stalked along
in front of me, once or twice stopping to listen
carefully. As we approached the head of the gorge
we became very quiet indeed – I knew that Gamal
must really believe what I had told him. Then we
were in sight of the place where the gorge, that
huge split in the surface of the earth, began. We
stole lightly across to the rock that overlooked
the gorge and stared downwards. All was just

as I had seen it! I was about to gloat over this,
when I glanced to one side. A hundred paces away
two robber scouts were staring intently at us and
beginning to move in our direction!

'Gamal!' I hissed. 'Run. Run!' Both of us turned
back to the wood and ran, fleet of foot, driven by
the sound of the robbers crashing through the
undergrowth behind us. Our only hope was the
two horses tethered where we had left them. In
spite of our start the robbers were not very far
away at the moment when we both leaped into
our saddles and urged our horses away. Catching
our panic they took off at speed, manes and tails
flowing in the wind. I looked round once and
saw one of the robbers about to fit an arrow into
his bow. I did not look again.

When we were back home Gamal was inclined
to be respectful of my gifts, but to wonder how it
was that if I had foreseen the robbers in the gorge
I could not also have known about the robber
scouts. I could not tell him.

'Can all women do magic?' he asked me.

'I don't think so,' I replied.

'Meroot can, you know,' he said.

'What kind?'

'I'm not sure. She won't talk about it. It's just
that I see her books and parchments. There's a
terrifying picture in one of them . . . And sometimes she mixes potions.' He sounded unhappy.

'I don't really understand magic,' I said truthfully. 'That's why I'm going to Euny's, I suppose.'

'Do you want to go?'

'I don't know.'

Somehow that day made me feel that I needed
to be taught whatever it was Euny knew. Perhaps,
I thought, she could teach me really effective

magic and I would be able to use it to make people do anything I wanted them to do. That was a pleasing thought. In any case, I felt myself moving inevitably towards her – even though I didn't like her much. It was very odd.

'So how is it,' Gamal persisted, 'that if you can see into the future you cannot beat me at chess? You should be able to see my moves several turns ahead.'

'I do beat you sometimes,' I said indignantly, but I saw his point. There was something that didn't make sense.

Now that I had discovered that Moon could speak I spent a lot of time talking to him, but to my disappointment he did not utter another sound. He would gaze at me very intelligently with his head on one side, or sit blinking his amber eyes, but that was all.

'Please say something, Moon,' I would beg. 'I know you can.' But he simply ruffled up his feathers and blinked at me with those astonishing eyes.

That night I dreamed again of the hazel tree and the tunnel. This time whatever was pursuing me was close at hand. When I woke up the feeling of fear was very great, though it was gradually succeeded by a longing for the hazel tree. I knew that something had to change, but I could not imagine what it might be.

Chapter Four

The Journey

One morning, however, I woke at dawn, shivering and sweating from my dreams, the tears pouring down my cheeks, and for the first time I knew what I must do. I got straight up out of bed, and began to prepare a bundle for myself. I put in two of my simplest smocks and chose another to wear, with a large pocket which would accommodate my owl (he had always enjoyed travelling in there). I included a bone comb that had been a present from my mother, sandals and a cloak. I wrapped a shawl round my shoulders, and put on the boots I wore in wet weather. I was very tempted to leave without saying goodbye to my parents or Erith but I feared that if I did so there would be a hue and cry in search of me. So I sat down to wait until the rest of the household was awake.

My parents were breakfasting when I entered their apartments. Erlain looked distressed as I told her that the day of my departure had come, yet all the same I believe she thought that I was right to go.

'We shall miss you,' she said, 'but I shall think of you every day. Be my brave girl and learn whatever Euny can teach you. And remember, it is only for a year and a day. Not *such* a long time.' It seemed a very long time to me. My father kissed me warmly, but said little. I felt that he did not like the parting, yet trusted Euny and her conviction that I needed to learn from her.

The person who made the greatest fuss was Erith, who wept and hugged me and wrung her hands in a truly heartbreaking way.

'I'm coming *back*, Erith,' I kept explaining, but she did not seem to think that helped at all. In the end I gave up trying to comfort her – it only made *me* want to cry. I picked up my bundle and simply walked out the door. Once safely away from the Wooden Palace, I felt much more cheerful; it was very pleasant walking along in the morning's cool. There was an autumn bite in the air which made me move quickly, but I felt full of energy, as if I could walk for ever. After about an hour I heard the sound of hoofs behind me on the track and looking back I saw Gamal following me. When he got closer I could see that he was angry but trying to hide it.

'You went away without saying goodbye to me.'

'I am sorry, but I only decided to go this morning, and by then I knew you would be out on the field practising. I asked Erlain to say goodbye for me.'

'She did, so I just left the field. Old Talan's in a rage.'

I thought he was rather brave. Meroot had punished him severely the last time he had run away from his tutors to ride with me.

'I'll have to go back, but I was determined to say goodbye.' He slid off his horse and he gave me an awkward boyish kiss. 'I hope you'll be happy with Euny. She looks a bit of an ogress to me.'

'I'll miss you.'

Unable to think of anything else to say, Gamal mounted his horse and soon disappeared home. I missed him the moment he was out of sight; now, instead of feeling light and exhilarated as I had when I set out, I felt sad and lonely. I continued my journey more slowly.

As the day wore on it became hot – a dazzling September day. After I had walked for several hours my feet became sore and I took off my boots and walked in the dust which felt silky and comforting. Foolishly, I had not thought to bring any water with me, so I drank out of the wayside streams. Later, however, I became very hungry and wondered why I had forgotten to bring bread. I found a few berries.

I was not very sure of the way but I had a sort of landmark. Once, on a trip I had made with him, my father had pointed out to me an odd-shaped hill in the distance. 'That's where Euny lives,' he had said. I could see the hill, purple-black, away in the distance, a hill that rose sheer out of a flat landscape. Sometimes I lost sight of it as I passed through woods or along deep leafy tracks but then it would re-appear and I would know that I was not lost. For a long time, though, it did not seem to get any closer.

In the late afternoon I came to a great forest which lay between me and the hill. I knew that forests were dangerous for unarmed travellers – that there might be boars or wolves or outlaws who lived there, and I feared being eaten or killed and robbed. I sat down in despair on the edge of the forest and wondered what to do. It would be a sad end to my journey to die in the forest – I was much too young to die, I thought.

Despite my fears I found it very beautiful in the forest, with the tawny autumn colours glowing like fires, and away in the distance the dim blue light of the dying day. I had discovered one of the broad rides which ran through the forest and it seemed to me that if I stuck to that (and it was going in the right direction), I might be safe, though once when I heard someone approaching I hid in the bushes. It was a party of monks and I thought of coming out and asking for their protection, but then it occurred to me they might disapprove of Euny so I stayed in my hiding place. It was growing cold in the forest and I shivered in my shawl. I knew that it would be dark before long and I fervently wanted to be out of the forest before nightfall.

Just as if I was being taken care of, I stepped out of the forest as the first stars were coming out. It was on a track which led straight towards the mysterious hill. I walked on, very tired now, the hill slowly looming larger between me and the sky, yet still a long way off. I thought I could hear the distant grumble of the sea. I was stiff from the walk, my legs were scratched and bleeding, I was cold and my bundle felt heavy, yet I kept going, one foot before the other. I sang to myself to keep up my spirits and looked up at the great stars above me. Suddenly, as if time had compressed itself, I stood at the foot of the great hill. Now, I thought, if I walked round it I should find Euny's house.

This was not as easy as it sounds. There were deep ditches and streams, little coppices, and high walls of bushes. Although I could dimly see the stepping stones over the stream I was so tired that I stumbled right into the stream and fell down full-length in the water. I gasped at the bitter cold, and then staggered out, my clothes dripping, and my flesh shivering in the night wind. I was past crying, simply trying to endure in order to reach Euny. When I drew poor little Moon out of my pocket he was ruffling his wet feathers indignantly. I thought it might make him cross enough to say something, but he did not speak. Nor did he speak when, a bit later, I fell heavily down a bank, hurting my ankle and scraping my arm.

'Euny! Euny!' I had begun to say out loud. It was just then that a crescent moon swung into view over a clearing and in its gentle light, black against the sky and the curve of the hill, I saw a little hut, with firelight showing under the door. I did not know whether it was the house I sought, but I knew that I could go no further. I stumbled towards it, pressed the latch, and the door swung open on a small square room. Between me and the fire was a rocking-chair with someone sitting in it who did not turn round.

'So Juniper decided to come after all, did she?' said Euny's voice. 'Shut the door behind you – there's a terrible draught.'

Chapter Five

Euny

Shivering and exhausted I crept towards the fire as an animal would have done and sank down before it. I must have looked a terrible sight – my hair and clothes sopping wet, my limbs covered in blood and mud, my ankle beginning to swell. If Euny had uttered one word of sympathy I would have burst into floods of tears. Instead she sat in silence, perfectly still. After a bit she said, 'There's a blanket on the bed,' and eventually it occurred to me that she meant me to strip off my damp clothes and wrap myself in it. I looked round the room – there was a box-bed in one corner and I went over and took out the ragged blanket and put it round my cold shoulders. Meanwhile Euny had filled a bowl with soup from the fire and set it in the hearth for me.

I put a hand out of my blanket, grasped the battered spoon she gave me, and ate the soup. It had odd bits of gristle in it and the strange flavour that I was to discover that Euny's soups often had, but it sent a shiver of delight through me. It was hot and spicy and I could feel some faint flicker of energy return to my exhausted body.

'There won't be much food to eat here,' Euny said, 'so you needn't expect it.'

What I was wondering at that moment was where I was going to sleep. I had always slept in a bed with down pillows and linen sheets. I could see there would be no room for me in Euny's tiny bed.

'Please, where shall I sleep?' I asked at last.

'On the hearth, of course,' said Euny. 'This isn't a palace, you know.' She managed to inject a lot of scorn into that remark. She got up, went across the room and fetched a furry skin. It had an odd smell which I didn't like at all.

'This will keep you warm,' she said.

Now I had another problem. Every night of my life Erith had helped me off with my clothes, brushed my hair, and tucked me into bed. Every morning she had bathed me, dressed me, and plaited my hair for me. I had no idea how to do any of it for myself. It had not occurred to me that anyone dressed and undressed without help.

'Please will you help me undress?' I asked.

Euny laughed, a bark of a laugh, not altogether unkind, and without a word went back to her seat in her rocking-chair. I realized, with astonishment, that she had no intention of giving me any help. With humiliating difficulty I managed to get my clothes off and comb my hair. I remembered that the little owl was still in my pocket and I took him out, stood him on a beam and fed him a titbit of mouse I had brought from home. I was nervous that this would provoke further rudeness from Euny, but to my surprise a broad smile spread across her face.

'How just like you!' she said, as if she was laughing at a private joke. Since she scarcely knew me I could not see how she knew whether it was like me or not.

Later I lay curled up in Euny's fur rug, half of it beneath me protecting me from the cold of the flagstones, half of it above me. Now that I was inside it the smell was overpowering. My head lolled uncomfortably on one of the creature's paws. There was warmth from the fire, though the shifting of the ashes disturbed me at first. Tired as I was I went quickly to sleep but woke long before dawn, cold and miserable, and hating the sound of Euny's snore from across the room. It seemed to me that I might have made a terrible mistake − that, although she had told me to come, Euny was not glad as I had expected her to be. In any case, I would never survive the discomfort and squalor of life there, with no-one to dress me and take care of me. Great tears of self-pity ran down my cheeks.

I sat up, my body cramped and frozen. It was not light yet but I could leave as soon as it was dawn. My torn smock, hanging over the rocking-chair near the fire, had dried in the night. I had simply to dress and leave before Euny woke. Just then, however, my ankle jarred with pain as I moved. I could see that, badly swollen as it was, I would never manage the long walk home. I groaned and curled back again into the strong-smelling skin.

I must have dozed because the next thing I knew was that it was light, I could hear Euny moving around, and smell ham frying.

'Thought you'd be hungry this morning,' said Euny. 'This is the last of the old pig − it's a bit high, but it'll do you good. We'll kill the next pig before winter.' She handed me a plate − it didn't look like a very clean plate to me − with a bit of fried ham on it and a hunk of black bread. She was quite right, I *was* very hungry, and although the ham had a rancid taste I gulped it down, together with the black bread and some lumpy porridge she was stirring over the fire.

'I can see you'll eat me out of house and home,' Euny said in her cross voice. 'Get dressed, wash yourself, comb your hair, try to look like a human being even if you can't look like a princess.' Obediently, though very slowly and awkwardly, I washed myself clean in the freezing water, combed my tangly hair, put on another of the smocks in my bundle and tied on my sandals. I was surprised to find that I could do it all by myself.

'Now sit down,' said Euny. 'We need to talk.'

Stiff and tired from my long walk and my night among the ashes, and still rather hungry, I sat miserably down, my swollen ankle in front of me.

Before we talked Euny selected some herbs, and tied them around my ankle.

'Walk on it,' she said, 'but not too much.' It hurt badly with each step I took.

'Now,' she said. 'I expect you feel very hard done by this morning, living in this miserable hole after the splendours of the palace.' She sounded as if she was gloating and I was too angry to trust myself to speak. Children in my country are trained to be very polite to grown-ups.

'But I am a poor person – not rich like your father – and this is the way poor people live.' (I knew, because Erlain had told me, that Euny had been offered a house at the Wooden Palace, and all kinds of presents by my father, but that she always refused.) As if she guessed my thoughts, Euny went on, 'I find life easier this way.

'Let me tell you why I think you are here. I shan't talk much about it after today, so listen carefully. What I know about is power. Not the sort of power your father has with soldiers and armies and weapons, but a power that comes from knowing . . .'

'I know a lot,' I said, eager to please. 'I know Latin, and about the stars, and mathematics, and poems . . .'

'Not that sort of knowing,' she said interrupting me rather contemptuously. 'That sort just gets in the way – makes you think you are clever, like weapons make men think they are strong. My sort of power is about *seeing* – seeing into the future, seeing into someone's heart and mind. Sometimes it is about knowing what a tribe or people must do to escape danger. Sometimes it is just about understanding yourself, or one other person. Seeing and knowing – and being very truthful about what you see and know – they make things begin to happen, maybe more things than battles and armies. Sometimes they prevent bad things.' I thought of the moment with Gamal on the hillside but did not feel like mentioning it.

'So could I have power?' I asked.

'It is too soon to say. It is possible. But you may spoil it.'

'How?' I asked anxiously.

'By wanting it too much. Or by using it badly.'

'And if I don't spoil it?'

'Then you will become what the powerful ones call a *doran*. And that might be very important for your father and his kingdom. But it is a long,

44

difficult path and it may be too much for you.'

'It won't,' I said, determined not to miss my chance.

'Or you may decide you don't like the idea when you know more about it.'

I thought that was very unlikely. I remembered Gamal's question.

'Is it only women who become *dorans*?' I asked her.

'No. But there are more women who take that path. Men prefer to put their trust in weapons and fighting. They don't know it but it makes them weaker.'

Asking Gamal's question had reminded me of something else.

'Is Meroot a *doran*?' I asked Euny. Her face darkened and her lip curled with scorn.

'Meroot only uses magic to make other people do what she wants.'

I remembered my own fantasies of doing just that.

'Is that bad?' I asked timidly.

'It is wicked,' Euny replied with a terrifying emphasis. Then, with the air of one who has had more conversation than she is used to, she stood up and started to pack some bread into a basket before hoisting it on her back.

'I have work to do today,' she said, 'so you'll just have to stay here. Light the fire and make some soup for supper. I'm not sure whether I'll be back by nightfall.'

Chapter Six

The First Day

When Euny had gone I spent a little while sitting glumly in her rocking-chair, my sore ankle propped up in front of me. Now that I was alone I examined the room in more detail. There were the ashes of the fire and hanging above it the chain which held a griddle and a kettle. There also hung a large piece of mutton, left there to blacken in the peat smoke. That, and no doubt the tallow lamp made from mutton fat, were what gave the hut its unpleasant smell. Beside the fire was a basket of peats, a little brush for cleaning the hearth, the lamp on a shelf, and a small stool. In addition to the rocking-chair and the bed the room contained a rickety table and an upright chair, a rather dirty woven rug, a bowl and jug, some cups and plates on a simple dresser, a quern with meal spilling out of the top of it and a jug with some milk. In a corner stood a pile of wood with some sticks lying on the top, and a tinder box on the floor beside it. There were dried plants hanging from the ceiling, and the remains of the pig's carcass. Euny owned nothing, it occurred to me, that was not absolutely necessary to keep her warm or fed, and I thought with wonder of the way she had refused my father's offer of money and possessions. The books, the musical instruments, the goblets, the jewels, the fine clothes, to which I had been accustomed at home, seemed unimaginable here.

It was a sunny day and I limped out of the hut to look at the world outside. In front of it was a pleasing landscape of copses with the great forest beyond. Wandering a short distance from the hut I found a few blackberries. Turning suddenly to return to the hut I saw the hill, or tor, rising sheer behind the hut, a steep hill with sides which looked as if they had been carved. Euny's hut stood small and insignificant in its shadow. Beyond the hill and the hut was the shore. This morning the sea broke softly on the sand.

What was I to do with myself all day? Euny had gone and might not be back till the morrow and there was I, all alone with nothing at all to do, and only able to walk with difficulty.

As so often since the day out with Gamal I tried to talk to Moon, but he did not stir from his daytime sleep. I had never before lit a fire or attempted to cook but because I was cold and would soon be hungry again, I thought I had better learn how. I thought it might be easier to light a fire of wood than of peat. I placed some big pieces of wood in the hearth and struck at the flint. Even when the sparks fell on the dry pieces of moss I took out of the tinder box, the little fire-seeds gradually faded. I tried time after time, feeling more and more irritated. After a bit it occurred to me that the twigs might light more easily than the wood. This time I trans- ferred the moss to the twigs, the twigs sizzled a little, and I thought that maybe the fire would light, but still I did not succeed.

I sat back on the chair and looked despairingly at the cold hearth. Other people could light fires. Why was I so stupid? Then I remembered seeing servants at home sweeping up the ashes and carrying them away, and without much hope of it making a difference I took down my pyramid of wood, cleared away the ashes in a shovel that lay beside the hearth, relaid the fire, and repeated the procedure with the tinder box. This time, to my delight, the twigs flared up, making a generous blaze, and at length the wood caught alight. I felt very proud of myself.

There was still some soup left in a cauldron, and although it was only the middle of the morning I heated it up and ate it, with some black bread that I had found on the dresser. I noticed the same odd taste that I had noted the night before. I later discovered that Euny had a way of throwing whatever food she had into her soup, not just bread and herbs but cheese or meat or offal together with any herbs that came to hand. It did not always taste nice. But I should have to devise another soup for our evening meal.

My hunger appeased, I went out to look at the pig and the chickens. The pig was a huge black beast that lived in a sty behind the hut; its grunts and snufflings had disturbed me more than once during the night. The chickens' white feathers looked dirty and bedraggled, but I was glad to notice that several eggs were already lying inside the hen-house, and I carefully collected them. I saw Euny had been growing some beans and flax, and some bere corn. There were a couple of stunted apple trees with a few apples left on the boughs.

Time hung very heavily on my hands for the

rest of that day. I talked a bit to Moon, hoping, as always, that he would reply, or even give me some advice, but he merely blinked, and went back to sleep. Limping painfully, I drew some water from Euny's well, and washed out the smock I had worn the day before, hanging it over the chair to dry. I washed my hair too and let it dry in the noontide sunshine which was bright and warm. I carefully arranged the blocks of peat on the fire and loved the smell as the fire reached them. Mindful of the charge to make some soup I managed to persuade a little more meat from the pig's carcass, and added some water and some herbs and a little meal, but it was a poor thin broth. When darkness fell I ate the soup with a couple of the eggs and the rest of the black bread and some milk, reluctantly saving what was left of the milk for the next morning. Before going to bed I built up the fire as much as possible and, wrapping myself once more in the strange-smelling animal skin, I lay down before the hearth.

The fire threw alarming shadows on to the walls of the hut. The silence outside felt ominous to me. Except for the occasional scream of a rabbit caught by a stoat or a fox, I could hear nothing at all, but I imagined outlaws surrounding the hut preparing to break into it. Because of my fears, and the discomfort of the floor, I slept very badly – the shifting and sighing of the fire disturbed me. There was a growing feeling of cold as the night drew on. 'I don't like this at all,' I thought, 'no matter how much power I get out of it, nor how important it is to be a *doran*. I'd rather marry the son of a neighbouring prince, or even the son of one of the knights, as all the other girls do. That would be much better than spending my life cold and hungry in a place like this. As soon as Euny returns I will tell her and then when my ankle is better I will go back home.' Feeling that I had settled something I rearranged the skin again and sank into a sound sleep. I was woken several hours later by Euny lifting the latch and entering the hut.

Chapter Seven

The Second Day

Although I had decided so firmly to leave Euny, I found it difficult to get round to telling her about it, perhaps because I was a little afraid of her. Maybe too, I thought that some marvellous thing might still happen which would make it worthwhile to live there.

On the second morning when I woke up cold and stiff, Euny decided promptly that my ankle was better, though it felt far from better to me, and sent me out, before breakfast, to collect two buckets of water from her well, to gather sticks and relight the fire, to wash my face in the cold water, and comb my hair. All this before our very meagre breakfast of porridge.

'Please, what am I going to give Moon?' I asked her anxiously. At the Wooden Palace, I had always begged the contents of the mouse-traps from the cook, or she had given me other scraps left over from our meals.

'There are plenty of field-mice around here. Let him go and hunt for himself,' said Euny. I looked anxiously up at Moon. Suppose he starved because it did not occur to him to seek his own food?

Actually I was still fairly hungry myself, though trying hard not to notice it. I thought that we would now settle down to lessons as I would have done at home, only in something much more interesting, like spells, but it didn't turn out that way. After a brisk tidying-up of the hut (that is, *I* tidied it, while Euny looked on and made sarcastic comments), we went out for an interminable walk in which Euny was seeking roots for some medicine she wanted to make. It was a chill, windy day and we marched for hours over meadows and through woods. Every now and then, for no reason that I could see, Euny would point to a plant that looked like all the others and order me to dig it up. Some of them had deep, tough roots, which she insisted I must dig up intact. I had no tool apart from a stick and my fingers, and in no time my pretty nails were full of earth, and my hands and smock were filthy. The only time she spoke to me was to give me long explanations of what the roots were and what they might be used for, which I promptly forgot.

In contrast to Euny who walked lightly and quickly, looking about her as if everything was interesting and must be noticed, I shuffled along, sullen and miserable, until I began to take refuge in comforting day-dreams.

'How many birds?' Euny asked suddenly.

'How do you mean?'

'There was a row of birds sitting on a branch. How many?'

Of course I had no idea. I had not even seen the birds.

This unpleasant trick, I was soon to discover, was a favourite one of Euny's. She was given to precise, detailed questions. What colour was the roof? What colour *exactly* had the sky been?

What direction was the wind blowing from? What animals had I noticed? What were they? What flowers had I seen? She would ask, but I never knew the answer. It made me feel very silly.

What I was thinking about was not the number of birds nor the direction of the wind but the bliss of returning to the comforts of Castle Dore. I reflected that as the winter came on, life, which was already hard at Euny's, would become intolerable, with the cold, hard floor feeling even colder at night, and the hunger becoming even more painful. It would be lonely, too. I had only been with Euny a day and a half, and already I was missing Erith and my parents and other children to talk to. It was at this point that I remembered that, after all, it was Euny who had asked me to come, and I thought that perhaps, as I was her godchild, she held some affection for me that she found difficult to show.

'Did you ... sort of ... want me to come?' I asked her timidly in the middle of a dark forest. I hoped for some sort of declaration from her that she loved me and was pleased that I was coming to live with her.

'It's all one to me,' she said disappointingly.

But there was something even more fundamental that I needed to know, only I scarcely knew how to ask the question.

'I know what you said yesterday, but I still don't see how I ... what you ... what I am here for,' I got out at last. Euny gave a heavy sigh as if this was an unreasonable bit of curiosity on my part.

'Earth, air, fire, water,' she said, and stopped.

'Like my rhyme,' I said with interest, remembering my neck-charm.

'Well, there you are.'

I didn't seem to be anywhere.

'There are . . . things I can do,' I said. 'I can find water hidden underground, I can heal people – sometimes, I can see into the future, and once I thought I heard Moon speak.'

'Don't boast!' she said sharply.

'But what does it *mean*?'

'It means that you must do exactly what I tell you!'

To make it all worse it began to rain in the course of the afternoon, but in spite of that we did not make for home. Cold and wet, with the rain plastering my hair to my head, carrying the full basket of roots, hungry because we had not eaten since that meagre plate of porridge at breakfast, I stumbled along behind Euny, now with my mind fully made up. Tomorrow I would get up early, while Euny was still asleep, would grab my things and would set off for home. I might even leave my things behind, I reflected, in case collecting them should wake Euny. After all, there were plenty more clothes at home. I pictured Erith's rapturous welcome and all the sympathy I would get as I told my story, though I also felt a spasm of shame that I did not quite understand.

I was very tired now and the long day's walk had caused my ankle to swell again. It was dark by the time we got to our own forest, but Euny entered it without hesitation and kept up a steady pace that, exhausted as I was, I found hard to match. I could think of nothing but sleep – my former raging appetite had died down now. When we came out of the forest there was a moon which showed the stepping stones across the stream as bright as day. It swam huge and golden over the shoulder of the tor and outlined the roof of Euny's hut. This was magical enough – a scene so beautiful that in spite of my exhaustion I felt transfixed by it – but there was something more. Standing between the tor and the hut, its branches silvered by the moonlight, quivering a little in the night breeze, stood the hazel tree I remembered from my dreams. My tiredness and hunger forgotten, I stood still and stared at the tree, stammering with excitement.

'The hazel tree. The tree in the dream. It's *here*.'

To which Euny, to whom I had said nothing about my dream, replied, 'Well, of course. It's been here all along. You could have noticed it by daylight if you weren't so absentminded. You'll have to do better than that.' And she went on into the hut.

As I stood, still transfixed by my discovery, I heard the brush of wings overhead and looked up to see Moon, white and ghostlike, flying above me, seeking his food just as Euny had recommended.

'Moon!' I called to him softly, 'I have found the hazel tree!' At which he circled round me a couple of times in acknowledgement before continuing on his hunting trail.

Chapter Eight

Learning

And so my life with Euny began. She was an odd mixture of busyness and laziness. She did not care at all about the state of the hut and spent most of the day sitting in her chair in front of the fire, sometimes asleep, sometimes humming tunelessly, sometimes just still and quiet. Yet she had periods of extraordinary energy. Alone, or taking me with her, she would walk for long distances, as on that first dreadful day (walking so quickly that I found I was out of breath trying to keep up). Often she was making for a hill, a forest, a ring of trees or of stones. Once there she would search diligently for some particular spot – I could never work out where it was going to be – and having found it would spend perhaps an hour there, singing a wild tuneless song, muttering words which sounded like poems. Her eyes would be closed, her face set and concentrated. She smiled to herself quite often, but sometimes her expression would change to one of pain, and once I saw tears pouring down her cheeks. She never said anything to me before or after these occasions, just let me stand there, on whatever windswept hill or moorland we happened to be, shivering and rather frightened. I wanted to ask her to explain these times to me but I never had the courage.

Soon after my arrival we had climbed our own tor – its sides were steep and gaunt, like the ribs of a giant, and I arrived at the top with my heart pounding. I could see our tiny hut a mere speck at the bottom, and there was a wonderful view of forest and hill, with the tor of Glasweryn away in the distance and a village with its ploughed fields. On this occasion Euny neither laughed nor wept, but simply stood quietly. Then she led me to a small wattle-and-daub hut that stood on the crest of the hill. Within it, like a queen in a hovel, was an extraordinary carved and painted figure set in a kind of cave made of stone. Her face was black, her eyes dark and wild, and upon her head she wore a crown decorated with a moon and stars. Her gown was blue and red, and sitting upon her lap was a baby, awkward and doll-like. A wreath of hedgerow flowers – the last beautiful flowers of autumn entwined with berries – had been hung round her neck and others were strewn at her feet or thrust into little pots. At her feet was a well, its ancient wooden lid beautifully carved with flowers and animals. There were candles too, set round the rim of the well, one or two still alight, the others burnt out as if many people had visited the place and left a burning candle as a memento of their visit.

Euny, always so dry, so caustic, astounded me by suddenly prostrating herself on the floor, while I stood awkwardly by. When she got up I saw that her face was wet with tears. Then she opened the well, threw in the dipper on its long chain, drank a little of the water and replaced the dipper without offering any water to me. On the way back to the hut she was silent. Only when we had nearly reached it did she say sternly to me,

'You are not to climb the tor, nor visit the place of the Mother unless I tell you to.' Immediately I felt irritated and as if I might wish to do so, though that steep climb would not otherwise have been much of a temptation.

In fact, Euny was full of instructions about what I might and might not do. From the moment she woke me each day from my uncomfortable sleep, usually very early in the morning, she ordered me out to draw water, to grind meal, to blow up the fire, to make porridge, to gather sticks, to sweep, to feed the chickens and chop up scraps for the pig. I did not much mind doing these things since they helped us to keep warm or fed, or meant that the plates and pots were cleaner than when *she* washed them; it did annoy me, however, to see her sitting in her rocking-chair, not helping, while I swept, or cooked, or cleaned the ashes from the fire, or staggered in with the pails of water. It made me feel that I was her servant, which I didn't like at all. Once, on a bad day, I mumbled my resentment at her, and she replied, with one of her crows of glee, 'Yes, you are my servant. That is exactly what you are.' My only comfort was that I did at least keep the hut cleaner than she did, and that I soon learned to cook nicer meals.

The two most painful things about life with Euny, however, were cold and hunger. In my privileged life in the Wooden Palace there had always been a fire blazing on the hearth, and I had always been warmly dressed and well-fed. Life in the hut was very different. The thin walls did not keep in the warmth of our fire, and every night I woke up shivering, so that I felt tired and miserable next day. As the winter approached I went out gloveless, in all weathers, on my innumerable errands for Euny, and my cloak and boots, made for life at Castle Dore, were not thick enough to keep out the damp and the cold. Soon I had chilblains on both hands and feet which became very sore, and drove me half-mad with irritation whenever I did get warm. Euny showed no sympathy for my shivers or my chilblains. Once, when I complained, she said, 'You came here to make your life real. Cold, hunger, the hard floor to lie on – those are ways to know the world. They are your teachers.'

If they were my teachers, I reflected angrily, then they made me very miserable. Yet I could not help noticing when I next picked up my spoon to eat my soup that, since I had had almost no food all day, the soup tasted better than any soup I had ever eaten in my life. It was as if my whole body had suddenly come alive and was singing. The flavour of every bean, grain and vegetable in the soup spoke to me. Even the water I drank tasted wonderful. Was it just the purity of Euny's well, or was it that, desperately hungry as I was, my mouth was wonderfully alert to enjoy all that entered it?

Similarly, when I came in half-frozen from a series of trips to the well, there was a special kind of joy in letting the warmth of the fire steal through my cold body, though the torment of the chilblains spoiled it a little.

It also occurred to me that I had never noticed the change from autumn to winter as sharply as I did now. Before, I was dimly aware, as everyone is, of the falling of the leaves from the trees, the coming of the frost and the short, dark days. Now, partly perhaps because of my fear of cold and hunger, I noticed that no two days were the same, that as the year declined, there were changes of sky, and stars, and the behaviour of birds, that I had never known before.

Not, of course, that I was ever observant enough for Euny.

'What were the clouds like?' she asked, as ever, when I returned from an expedition. 'Did the wind change? What birds did you see? Which trees have lost all their leaves? What shrubs still have flowers upon them? What was the moon like?'

It had been my habit to walk through the world in a pleasant dream, remembering stories or conversations, going back over bits of the past I had enjoyed, or having romantic fantasies of the future. Euny did not seem to understand this at all.

'You are hopeless, hopeless,' she told me angrily. 'You will never make a *doran*.' I was wounded by this, and sulkily tried to remember to notice the sort of things she asked about, but she had an unnerving way, after I had made a point of counting the birds, or observing the clouds, of picking on something quite new – the shape of the landscape, the number of footpaths and the way they joined one another, the appearance of people we had met by the wayside, or animals. I tried harder, but it seemed to be no use at all.

In addition to hunger and cold, I realized that I was also struggling with silence. Euny sometimes went all day without addressing a word to me. In desperation I had long conversations with Moon, and with Borra, the pig, standing beside his sty and scratching his back with a stick.

Euny often fed Borra the best of the scraps and sometimes I stole one or two of them for myself before giving them to him. He, after all, was very fat, whereas I was much thinner than I used to be. I enjoyed Borra's grunts, but I would rather have talked to another person.

'Do you ever feel lonely?' I asked Euny once. There was a long silence.

'Sometimes,' she replied.

'Don't you mind?'

She made a gesture like pushing something away from her. 'I am used to it. It doesn't matter.'

When the chores were all done she expected me to sit still as she did, she in her rocking-chair, me on a cushion on the hearth. I hated doing this, and soon learned to spin out the chores so that they kept me busy for much of the morning, but sooner or later there was nothing for it but to go back into the hut, and sit down. Half a day would pass without conversation or movement. Sometimes I fell asleep – upright, since Euny saw no reason for me to lie down during the day. Always I yawned and fidgeted.

'It's very boring,' I said unwarily once.

'Good,' said Euny, and spoke no more. Not for the first time, I hated her. I spent the time dreaming of food.

There was something that I began to mind more than the cold and hunger. It was the feeling that while I was enduring all this discomfort and Euny's wounding sarcasm, I was learning nothing about the special sort of power that was the gift of the *doran*. I had supposed that Euny would sit me down and instruct me properly in the use of herbs and ointments, helping me to understand, as all my other teachers had done, instead of merely tossing off a comment about a plant now and then, but when I saw Euny working on her medicines and asked for information, she would wave me away with, 'It's not important,' as if the whole thing was a secret, and suggest that it was time for me to get on with feeding the pig.

'How shall I learn if you never teach me anything?' I asked crossly one day. She did not bother to reply.

Chapter Nine

Borra

The worst thing that ever happened in the first part of my stay with Euny, however, was the day she spent a long time sharpening the big knife on a stone by the door, and then handed it to me.

'Go on,' she said to me, and I gazed at her in puzzlement.

'The pig,' she said. 'Kill it!'

I stared open-mouthed at her, looking from her face to the gleaming knife in her hand.

'I couldn't possibly,' I said. I remembered the horrors of pig-killing in the farms around Castle Dore – the squeals and the flowing blood. I had always shuddered and hurried by, back to the life of a princess.

'Someone has to do it!' said Euny. 'So why not you?'

'Please don't make me,' I begged her. (Already my experience of Euny should have taught me that that was the worst possible way of going about things.)

'I have noticed that you like to eat pig meat,' she said haughtily. 'The old carcass is empty. If you don't kill this pig there will be no meat for you to eat.'

'You don't mean it!' I said. Fat bacon was most

of our diet. I knew she did mean it. Furious with her, I snatched the knife out of her hand and went to the pigsty.

Borra had become a good friend of mine by now. At the sound of my footstep he looked up expectantly. I hid the knife behind my back and talked kindly to him, noticing the life in the bright little eyes, the pleasure in his grunts. I went back to Euny.

'I can't do it!' I said, throwing down the knife. 'It's cruel!'

'So we shall starve to death!' she said triumphantly, as if the prospect pleased her.

I tried to argue with her. 'I don't understand. I thought the *dorans* loved the creatures of the world and wanted to care for them.'

'What could show more love for an animal than eating it?' replied Euny.

'But you are taking its little life away from it. All it has.'

'For it to become part of the life in you. You are being false. What you will discover – *if* you ever stop being interested in yourself for long enough to notice the world around you – is that all life feeds off other life.'

'But not Borra! He's so sweet, and I love him so much that I cannot kill him.'

'But sweet or not you would eat him if I killed him. Is that not right?'

Shame-faced, I was forced to nod. I knew that I had only to smell bacon cooking to feel a wild hunger.

'So long as *you* don't have to feel responsible for killing him. So long as the princess does not get blood on her hands! Wonderful!'

Euny's scorn hurt me, but I minded it even

more when she picked up the knife and handed it back to me.

'Hurry up! There is a lot of work to be done on the carcass, and we need to start while there is still plenty of daylight.'

I left her again, but instead of going back to the sty I began to pace round the bottom of the tor. I had never been spoken to in my life in the way Euny spoke to me, and it left me helplessly angry. It was then I noticed what I was doing with the knife – brandishing it furiously in the air – and suddenly I observed, with a faint glimmer of unexpected amusement, that what I was doing in my mind was plunging the knife into Euny. I couldn't kill a pig, but I had a secret longing, at least just for that moment, to kill Euny. Stiffening myself for the horrid task, knowing that my future as a *doran* was linked to my obedience to Euny, I went and killed the pig, without thinking about it, praying to Borra's spirit to forgive me.

White, shaking, covered in blood, I went back to the hut. For a second I was too upset to notice that Euny was not alone, indeed that the hut seemed to be full of people. There was my mother looking her most beautiful, her delicate pale face framed in a collar of fox. There was Erith, shocked at the sight of me. There was Gamal standing by the hearth regarding me sympathetically, and beside him another boy of about our own age who stared at me in open amusement. I stood there looking mutely at them, blood-stained, my hair falling over my face, the knife in my hand. My mother made a small, stifled exclamation as she caught sight of me and then was silent. Erith was less restrained.

'You look awful,' she said.

'I've killed the pig,' I said unnecessarily to Euny, not knowing what else to say. Euny, quite unruffled by the company, nodded with a small, pleased expression, took the knife from me and suggested that I should change my smock. Gamal, trying to act as if all was as usual, introduced me to Finbar, a new page at my father's court who had come to carry food and warm clothes that my mother and Erith had prepared for me. Even in the circumstances I noticed that he was a very handsome boy, with brilliant blue eyes and black hair. As I tried to speak to my mother, Finbar, where she could not see him, was pointing at me, and silently pretending to hold his sides with laughter, like a mocking jester behind the throne. I thought he was the rudest boy I had ever met.

Later, my hair combed, and wearing a cleaner smock, I walked with my mother to the foot of the strange-shaped hill. A jumble of feelings fought inside me – humiliation at being caught looking so dreadful, anger with Euny for making me kill the pig, triumph at finally having done it, apprehension about what my mother would say. Would she persuade me to return to Castle Dore? I realized I had very mixed feelings about that.

For a long time neither of us spoke.

'So how is it?' my mother said at last.

I mumbled some reply, but could not speak for the sob in my throat.

My mother stood for a long time looking up at the steep sides of the hill, as if trying to read something from it. The she said, 'Of course, you must come home if it is too dreadful. But, I don't know, I have a feeling that you want to be here. Awful as it is.'

An extraordinary surge of gratitude ran through me, gratitude that although she was my mother, she could see and understand something that went beyond my thinness, my swollen fingers, and my own anger and perplexity. I began to cry in earnest because of her love for me, and she put her arms round me.

'Why do I have to?' I asked her.

'I don't know.'

'I felt so ashamed,' I said, 'that you and Erith and the boys saw me all blood-stained from killing the pig. And that Euny and I live in such poverty.'

She lifted up her white profile and looking like the daughter of a prince, which she was, said, 'You were always a brave child, Ninnoc. Knowing you, I expected you would live this ordeal with courage. Life with Euny is hard, but it won't go on for ever.' She smiled at me. 'Don't despair.'

'I don't understand it,' I said, 'but I seem to need to be here. And yet it *is* awful.'

'One good thing,' went on Erlain, 'we have brought you some food, some sacks of wheat and oats. That should help. That and the pig.' She smiled at me again. 'And Erith put in some blankets and pillows and a thick woollen cloak.'

'Good,' I said.

'Gamal has brought you some cakes and some wine. You should get a decent supper tonight.'

'You do understand,' I said in gratitude.

I was humbled by my mother's generosity, at her willingness to let me, her only child, follow a strange path. I flung my arms round her again and this time we both wept.

I also had time to talk with Gamal.

'I shall come and see you sometimes,' he said. 'And so will Finbar. He's become a good friend. I'm teaching him our language – you know his home is on an island a long way north of England. He wants to be a navigator.'

I felt a pang of jealousy at Gamal's transparent enthusiasm for his friend.

'I don't like Finbar,' I said. 'I think he is very rude.'

'You'll like him when you know him better. Everybody likes him. He's awfully funny, and he's brave.'

It was impossible to ignore Finbar completely when the party left. I held out my hand coldly to him, and he kissed it, as was the custom, still taunting, it seemed to me, with those mocking eyes.

'I hope *you* will come again, Gamal,' I said pointedly.

I felt very lonely when they had all gone away and I was back alone with Euny again, but I had no time to dwell on it since Euny and I spent the rest of the day cutting up the pig – a tiring and messy business – so that it could be salted. We did cook some of it at once, though, and had a marvellous supper which I ate ravenously.

'We shan't starve this winter,' said Euny with satisfaction, looking at the sacks stored in the corner of the hut.

'What did you do in other winters?' I asked curiously.

'Survived,' said Euny shortly.

'The trouble with being hungry or cold,' I said thoughtfully, 'is that you think of nothing else.

It's like having a pain. On the other hand you really appreciate it when there is food to eat or a warm fire. I never knew food to taste so good as it has done these last few weeks.'

Euny grunted.

'I didn't know I could kill anything,' I said, still minding about Borra, even though he tasted very good.

Euny smiled a wrinkled, leathery smile that I had never seen before.

'You were a good, obedient girl,' she said.

'You didn't give me much choice,' I replied crossly.

'I am proud of you,' she said, and I could scarcely believe my ears.

Chapter Ten

Angharad

One day Euny said, 'Tomorrow we go to see Angharad of the West.'

'Who is she? Where does she live?'

'A long journey. You'll see.'

'But suppose Gamal comes to see me while I'm gone.'

'He'll just have to go home again, won't he?'

It was a bright winter day when the two of us set off, with the sun winking on icy puddles and the sky blue and clear. The air seemed to sparkle. The prospect of a change had cheered me up and I felt happier than I had done for some time, even though Euny insisted on walking extremely fast. By now Moon was too big to fit in even the largest pocket and I carried him in a special bag I made for him out of an old shift.

My warm cloak was very comforting, but my boots felt too small for my swollen toes. I could feel the cold of the ground through the soles as they slipped and slithered, my hands quickly became blue and numb, and even with an old ragged blanket of Euny's round my head and shoulders I could feel the wind biting me. Euny, as usual, seemed not to notice the cold at all.

'Don't dawdle, girl,' she said, whenever I paused

for breath. We had not brought much food with us, just some bread and some withered apples.

Much later we stopped at a farm and Euny begged some milk. The farmer's wife was baking hot rolls and the air was filled with the delicious smell of new bread. She picked out two rolls each and gave them to us. Seeing my wan face and frozen hands she asked us into the fire and then she suggested that it was too late to go on that night and that there was hay enough in the barn to keep us warm. I slept well that night in deep gratitude for her kindness, though Euny roused me from a sound sleep before it was light and insisted that we must be on our way. Rosy from the nest of the hay, my chilblains itching at the unaccustomed warmth, I stumbled out yawning, ate my second roll and drank the rest of the milk and set off again.

On this day we walked along a huge sea channel, a giant estuary, like a sea itself. From the cliffs we could see dangerous rocks below – the ships stayed well out in the centre. The blue-grey colour of the sea was shot with white, like a ripped garment with its lining showing through.

Sustained by a good night's sleep and a breakfast, I found that I walked faster and incurred fewer rebukes from Euny, though the endless catechism about what I had seen on the walk – 'How many boats?' and so on, continued. She had spoiled the pleasure of walking for me, filling it with anxieties about noticing and remembering. I did seem to be a little better at it than I had been, however.

By that evening, to my distress, we were miles from any human habitation. We drank water from a stream, but we had nothing to eat and

I was bitterly hungry. When it grew too dark and I was too tired for us to walk any further, we sat on a log in a wood and simply waited for the night to pass. I took Moon from his travelling bag and watched with envy as he swooped over the moorland in search of food.

'I'm hungry,' I said accusingly, and then, when no reply was forthcoming, 'Why didn't we prepare properly for this journey? We could have brought more bread with us, maybe some beer.'

'But then you miss the pleasure,' said Euny.

'What pleasure?'

'Of living as birds do from the hand of Providence.'

I thought of the starving birds I had often found lying dead on the ground in winter.

'Birds often die at the hand of Providence.'

'Sometimes. Mostly not.'

I listened to the ravening eagle inside me demanding to be fed.

'I must have food,' I said desperately.

'If there is no food, you simply have to be hungry.'

'Don't you mind being hungry?'

Euny hesitated.

'Nowadays, not at all. It is like the weather – I live with it. But when I was a child . . . yes, I wept a great deal about being hungry . . .'

I was intrigued. Euny had never before told me anything about her past – I am not sure that I thought she had one, that she had not emerged into the world fully-grown, wearing her greeny-black clothes. I hoped she would say more, but she did not, and I did not dare to press her.

'Tell me where we are going?' I asked at last to distract myself from all my discomforts.

'To one of the greatest *dorans* in the land — Angharad of the West. This country, you know, has many women of power but she is one of great power, and she has offered to teach you.'

'What sort of power will I have?'

'We will know when you are ready for it . . . *if* you are ever ready for it, because you are very slow and stupid. When you can use it rightly.'

That night seemed interminably long, and it was dreadful to have to set off walking again. My feet were now so swollen that I could only hobble along with difficulty. My hunger had mysteriously vanished as it does when no food is in prospect, though I felt quite weak and occasionally a little faint. We paused only once, to drink water from a spring.

Then, in the late afternoon, we breasted a hill overlooking the sea, and Euny pointed to a little house set in the valley, with the sparkling waters of a lake behind it. Smoke was rising from the smoke hole and there was something about the house that was pleasing and reassuring. I quickened my painful steps.

When we got nearer I could see something brightly-coloured hanging over the stone wall. There were patches of vivid red and yellow and green, but I was almost too tired to wonder about them, still less to ask questions.

It took us a while longer to reach the house and by the time we did so it was nearly dark. Euny lifted the latch, we entered a shadowy fire-lit room, in which Angharad, a woman of graceful middle age, rose to greet us. The room was deliciously warm, with a large fire. There was the scent of a rich, meaty stew in the air.

I unwrapped the blanket from my head and

stood uncertainly in the soft fire-light, feeling as if I might burst into tears. The room swirled disturbingly about me just when I wanted so much to look at it, I had a horrible feeling that I was going to be sick, and then I was aware of Angharad catching me as I fell.

When I came to from my faint, Angharad was very gently easing the boots from my swollen feet.

'When did you last eat?' she was asking Euny.

I was aware at once of the comfort and refinement of life in Angharad's house and felt ashamed of my dirty clothes and the ragged blanket. But Angharad showed no sign of despising us. When I felt better it was lovely to be drawn forward to the fire – though the heat caused my toes to itch furiously – to sit in a comfortable chair, and to fill my hungry stomach (my appetite had sprung back to life at the first sniff of the stew).

There was a sort of step around the hearth with cushions on it, and a big chair. In one corner stood a loom strung in brilliant colours, and in another corner a ladder passed up into a shadowy chamber. The chair, the table and the cushions were covered in bright fabric, in the palest pink, rosy orange, a deep inky blue, all of them glowing like jewels in the half-dark of the firelight. The colour, the comfort, the rich taste of the soup I was drinking, could not have been more different from the hardships of Euny's house. There was also a smell of roses, one that I would later know seemed to pervade Angharad's house. I can never smell a rose to this day without remembering her.

Angharad, wearing a pretty red gown, with her shining fair hair, and her gently apple-cheeked face, was not in the least like Euny. She reminded me a little of my mother, and I was instantly drawn to her. While she talked to Euny – a conversation about people who were unknown to me – I was aware of her readiness to include me, the way her grey eyes turned to me and smiled at me with a sympathy to which I had grown unaccustomed. At the same time her hands were busy with her spindle. Gradually I grew warmer and relaxed on my cushion, but was immediately aware of a desperate need to sleep. Suddenly Angharad interrupted the conversation with Euny and stood up.

'Come!' she said to me. 'You are tired out.'

She picked up a candle-holder, lit the candle from the fire, and led the way up the ladder. Above were two chambers, a big one and a small one. She took me to the small one, where there were two beds upon the floor, palliasses filled with straw covered with brightly-coloured blankets, and pointed to the one that had a thin white sleeping shift folded upon it. She left me; I undressed, settling Moon comfortably on a beam, and I crept into the nest of rustling straw. Then Angharad came back, carrying bandages and a jar of ointment. She tended the open sores on my feet. She tucked the blankets around me and kissed me gently.

'I hope you'll be very happy in my house!' she said. Then the waves of sleep were lapping round me.

Chapter Eleven

Spinning the Thread

I was woken by a voice saying insistently, *'Please wake up. I want to talk to you.'* With a start I came to, saw sunlight brilliant on the white walls of the room, and could not think where I was. I turned my head and saw a girl of about my own age, a very pretty girl, sitting cross-legged by the bed, watching me intently. She had long fair hair, plaited, falling down over her shoulder, and her eyes were a vivid green.

'Who are you?' I asked in surprise.

'Trewyn,' she said. 'I live with Angharad. I'm her apprentice. Didn't they tell you about me?'

It seemed useless to explain that Euny never told me anything, so I simply smiled at her.

'I'm longing to talk to you,' she said, full of eagerness. 'Angharad said you were a princess!'

I must confess that I felt pleased that Trewyn was obviously impressed by this, but I still felt too shy to launch into a long description of my life.

'Do you sleep in here too?' I asked, seeing the other bed disarranged.

'Yes. I'm so pleased you are here. I was longing to wake you up and talk to you when I got home last night – I was out looking for a plant Angharad needed to make a dye. But she wouldn't let me wake you up.' She paused for a moment. 'Are you hungry?' I nodded.

She got up and went out of the room, and for a moment I caught sight of her lovely profile and long neck – it was she and not I who looked like a princess, I thought. I lay back, propped on my pillow, still quite tired, but enjoying the warmth of my bed, the simple lines of the room, and the fact that, for the first time in months, I was to have a companion of my own age.

In a little while she was back with an oatcake, and a drink they make in those parts, fermenting the whey of the milk. The good plain taste of the oatcake – delicious like all Angharad's cooking – and the fiery warmth of the drink, put new energy into me. While I ate Trewyn asked about Moon and tried to talk to him, but he blinked stupidly at her.

I climbed back down the ladder to the room where the two *dorans* were sitting in front of the fire together. Euny, usually so pale, looked a little flushed from the fire. She looked up at me, saying, 'Tomorrow I will travel north.' My face fell at the thought of setting forth once more into the winter landscape on my sore feet, as well as leaving Trewyn and Angharad's comfortable house, but Angharad said quickly, 'But you will be staying here.' I turned in surprise to Euny who said, 'I will be gone for two months. Angharad will teach you in that time.' The pleasure must have shown in my face because she said, rather crossly, 'I hope she won't spoil you too much.'

'Nonsense!' said Angharad. 'She's a sensible girl, and she and Trewyn will be company for one another. Come back and fetch her in the spring.'

*

I think my obvious preference for Angharad must have rankled with Euny. The next day I walked a little way with her on her journey. Then she stopped.

'Go back now.' She hesitated. 'You think I am hard on you, maybe that I do not care about you. I can only be a *doran* in the way that is natural for me.' Euny waited, as if she was trying to say more, but could not manage it, and then she kissed me, roughly, on the cheek, turned and marched away. I was touched by her speech, but could not wait to get back to Angharad and Trewyn.

One of the reasons that Angharad had offered to keep me for a while, I think now, was that she believed Euny was starving me and wanted to feed me up. The food was generous, delicious, and she encouraged me to enjoy it, occasionally saying things like, 'Young girls need proper nourishment,' which I took to be an oblique criticism of Euny. Not that I felt she disliked Euny.

'You have one of the most remarkable *dorans* in the country as your teacher,' she said to me one day, when she and I were out gathering docks to make a green dye.

'How do you mean?' I asked with bitterness. 'What is it that is so remarkable?'

'Among the *dorans* we speak of people having power, you know. We don't mean power like kings or popes have power, of course, but power to bring things back into a sort of harmony, like tuning an instrument that's gone flat.'

'And Euny can do that?' I said disbelievingly.

'In a most unusual way, yes. She sees to the heart of things.'

There was something I wanted to say to

Angharad, only it was difficult to say it because it felt disloyal.

'She's very hard on me.'

Angharad was silent for a long while and then she said, 'Did Euny ever tell you the story of her life?' I shook my head.

'When Euny was a tiny little girl her parents were killed in a raid. Some of the tribes were very brutal in those days. They didn't just take cattle and crops . . . Some say that Euny's mother was killed in front of her – that she only escaped because she was hidden in the roof of the barn, but that she peeped out and saw what happened . . . Two or three of the children were left, but their house was destroyed and they had nowhere to go. They lived as they could, roaming the countryside, orphaned and homeless, begging food or work here and there, sleeping wherever they could be warm. Euny's whole childhood was like that. Only, when she was fourteen, a famous *doran* called Phrene took Euny in. She was starved and sick, like a little wild animal in winter, but Phrene was very gentle with her, and slowly Euny became strong and well. I know this' – Angharad gave me her sweet smile – 'because I was Phrene's apprentice, and Euny and I were sister *dorans*-in-training, just as you and Trewyn are. Phrene reckoned,' she went on, 'that Euny was the best pupil she ever had, and as you know, good *dorans* are made by good teachers. You will be a good, perhaps a great, *doran* partly because Euny trained you.'

'But she *doesn't* train me,' I said obstinately, although I was very moved by this tragic story.

'Child,' said Angharad slowly, and there was a long pause, 'open your eyes.'

79

When we were back in the house we boiled a vat of the dock leaves and vinegar and I pushed the skeins of white wool into it.

'Without the vinegar – what is called the *mordaunt* – ' Angharad said, 'the dye would run as soon as you washed the wool. It is the biting acid that makes the colour fast. It was brave of you to leave home and go and live with Euny. I know what Euny's housekeeping is like. You must often have been frozen as well as hungry.'

The pleasure of Angharad's sympathy made it possible to swallow my resentment.

'It was rather cold,' I admitted. 'But I wasn't really brave. I just couldn't help myself. Also I know that Euny has something to teach me . . . if she only would.'

Angharad turned and looked at me. 'Perhaps you think learning to be a *doran* is like learning French or mathematics. But it isn't. It's quite different.'

'But I've only got a year and a day,' I reminded her, 'and so far I haven't learned anything.'

'Well, after today you will have learned how to dye wool with dock leaves.'

Later, when we fished the shining green skeins out of the vat and hung them over the stone wall to dry in the sun, I had a sense of achievement, but thought, 'It's nothing to do with being a *doran*.'

Although Angharad fed me properly and kept me warm she expected me to work hard. To begin with she taught me how to tease wool, the process of preparing it for spinning. I learned to pull the wool off the fleece, take out the dirty and tangled bits, part the wool between my fingers until it was of even texture, and then comb it into delicate little rolls.

'It's the preparation that counts in spinning,' Angharad said. 'If you are lazy about that you will never spin an even thread.'

Then she showed me how to knot some thread on to the spindle, and, spinning it between my feet, twist the combed wool on to it while the spindle revolved. It was very difficult at first because the thread kept breaking and going into lumps. It was nothing like the perfect, even thread that Angharad made so rhythmically. I persisted, though, and eventually, to my great pride, a cone of spun wool rested on the spindle. Then, instead of letting me whirl the spindle between my feet, she stood a spinning dish on the floor beside me and I found I could spin much faster and more easily than before. I was delighted at first, then I got bored and began to spin more carelessly, wanting to be done with it. The result was rather poor. Angharad did not scold me, she simply expected that I would go on practising.

'Wool is a living thing,' she said once. 'That is why you cannot spin wool from a dead sheep.'

Watching her spin I noticed how, as she joined one piece of wool to another, the little hairs of the wool clung together to make a strong thread with no trace of a join. As we teased the wool plucked from the fleece I suddenly saw it with new eyes, noticing the tiny black flecks of peat in it, and the yellow waxy substance that made my hands soft. As we carded it and made it into long webs of wool I felt its softness, its delicate strength. Angharad's long, slim hands twirling the distaff and making a fine, even, thread made it seem almost as if she spun it out of herself. I caught myself trying to match her rhythm, to move into the kind of easy concentration that produced a thread without lumps, but I kept finding that either I tensed myself and squeezed the unspun wool so hard that it would not flow properly into the thread, or that I pulled the threads out so far that they thinned and broke. It was more difficult than I had thought at first.

'It's how you feel, isn't it?' I said to Angharad one day in a moment of insight. 'That's what makes the evenness of the thread. You need to concentrate, yet not to notice that you're concentrating.' I suddenly remembered what she had said about learning to be a *doran* being different from learning French.

'Do you think spinning could be helpful in learning how to be a *doran*?' I asked.

Angharad laughed.

'It's exactly the same thing,' she said.

I frowned.

'How can it be the same thing? Every old woman sitting spinning on her doorstep knows how to do this. They're not all *dorans*?'

'No, not all, but don't under-estimate their wisdom. When you are wise it won't make them stupid.'

Chapter Twelve

Making the Cloak

Life in Angharad's house could not have been more different from life with Euny. Gradually she taught me to dye with many different plants – with leaves and roots and berries. On almost every sunny day the wall was hung with wool in jewel colours – the pink, orange and red of madder and lichen, the blue and purple of woad, the yellow of dandelions, marsh marigolds and heather, each carefully set with its *mordaunt*. When I looked at the wool dyed a wonderful delicate yellow from lichen, I remembered with amusement the frustrating morning I had spent trying to collect urine from Betsy the goat – goat's urine being the best *mordaunt* for lichen.

Mornings were spent cleaning the house, drawing water, building a fire, preparing food, finding herbs, making and using dyes. In the afternoons the three of us sat down to our spinning, often whiling away the time with stories and songs. Trewyn and I would have an hour or two to ourselves in the late afternoon, and then after supper we returned to our spinning.

'When you have enough wool,' Angharad said to me, 'I shall teach you to weave.'

'What shall I weave?' I asked her.

Angharad nodded to Trewyn who left the room

and came back with a cloak over her arm. At a further signal from Angharad, Trewyn put the cloak on over her simple brown smock, and fastened it with a gold clasp. The cloak was a deep, dark green, lit here and there with a vivid flash of pink, a fish or a flower which floated in its dusky depths. Trewyn's slim body, her long neck and her beautiful profile with its perfect cheekbones seemed to take on a dignity and a mystery. Somehow the cloak seemed to reveal everything about her that I already knew as well as other things about her that I had only guessed at.

'This is the cloak of a *doran*,' said Angharad. 'Every *doran* has one, and it needs to be carefully made because one day it will be your protection against the magic of sorcerers. It must be as perfect as it can be.'

'Will mine be like that?' I asked, amazed that Angharad might think me capable of making such a cloak.

'No. It will be as you make it. When you thread the loom you will know which colours to use. That is why you need to prepare a good stock of colours now so that then you will have what you need.

I returned to my spinning with a new zeal, determined now to make the thread as perfect as I could. It reflected my mood continually – it broke when I was tired or angry or impatient, or flowed effortlessly when I was calm and happy. Angharad gave me a shelf on which to store the wool for my cloak, and every day I added to the coloured skeins.

It was a real relief to me that I was no longer cold or hungry. Even when our sleeping chamber grew cold on the frostiest nights, it was always possible to creep down and sit by the dying embers of the fire. And there was always enough food, though it was simple enough – milk and goat cheese, porridge, bread, beer. I was no longer tortured by chilblains, nor weary from hunger. It felt like a very precious sort of freedom.

One day Angharad said to me, 'It is time to start weaving now. You must choose the threads with which to make the warp of your cloth.'

I looked helplessly at the shelf with its many coloured skeins and balls of wool.

'I don't know how to choose,' I said lamely.

'Look inside yourself,' Angharad said. 'You do know really.'

I looked inside myself but no knowledge came, only a sort of panic.

'I don't know,' I said again. 'You choose.'

Angharad did not reply, but began moving around the house preparing supper. Trewyn was out on some errand of her own. Moon stared down at me from the beam above my head, at a time when he was usually out hunting for food. I sat, feeling bewildered at what was expected of me, and when supper came was grateful for the diversion. I turned to pick up my spindle, but Angharad shook her head.

'Weaving,' she said emphatically. I continued to sit on my stool, feeling silly. Much later Angharad and Trewyn rose to go to bed. Angharad looked at me, her gentle, motherly face unexpectedly determined.

'No point in going to bed till you've solved it,' she said. Trewyn threw me a sympathetic glance as the two of them left me there.

When they had gone I straightened my aching back and wondered what to do. I could, of course, sleep in Angharad's chair and she would be none the wiser, but this would bring me no nearer to solving my problem. I looked again at the wool on the shelf and felt more puzzled than ever. I stared at each colour in turn – the pinks, the reds, the oranges, the blues, the purples, the yellows, the browns, the greens, and tried to imagine beginning work with them, but none of them claimed me.

I wiped away a tear. I could see that I would still be sitting here at breakfast-time and that even Angharad, who was always kind, would sternly force me to wait until inspiration struck. I could, of course, just take up whichever colour came to hand and start work with that. Angharad would not know (or would she?) that I had cheated. Exasperated, as my hand hovered over the shelf, I thought that I might choose one of the colours blindfold.

Yet immediately it fell back again to my side. However tired I was, however hopeless it seemed, there was simply no point in cheating. If this cloak was somehow to be my protection it needed to be woven with truth. Both Euny and Angharad, so very different from each other, had taught me that.

For a few moments I felt lonely and rather cross, as if someone ought to be telling me what to do. The feeling of crossness grew and grew until I slapped the side of the loom in my rage. Why didn't my teachers help me? Almost at once, I saw the answer. It was that, like a small child taking its first steps, there was something I needed to try out, that only I could teach myself.

Now I was very still, trying to notice something in myself that I had never noticed before.

Sweating a little, with a sense of growing excitement, and trembling a little too, I heard myself suddenly say out loud, 'Who are you?' And then, quite firmly, I answered myself, as if I had never properly understood this before, 'You are Juniper.' As I said this, my hand, completely sure of itself, reached out and picked up wool of the deepest midnight blue and luminous grey-blue. My hand reached out again and this time, it took up white, undyed wool. On its third journey to the shelf it chose two yellowy colours – a deep amber and a lighter yellow. Did I really know that these were the 'right' colours? Yes, I did, but I did not know how I knew. I began reaching the midnight blue wool round the loom, knotting it, weighting it, too concentrated on what I was doing to find it odd that it was now the middle of the night. At one point, however, I looked up and saw that Moon's amber eyes were still fixed unwinkingly upon me. When Angharad got up to milk Betsy the next morning there were many threads on the loom. She came straight across the room to look, nodded with pleasure, and said, 'You got it right. I knew you would.'

Chapter Thirteen

To be a *Doran*

'Do you *want* to be a *doran?*' I remember Trewyn asking me one day as we sat high up in the branch of a tree.

'I want to *understand* all kinds of things,' I said. 'Maybe more than some people do. Or maybe they do it differently. And I don't want to be pushed into getting married just for the sake of it.'

'I'm a bit scared of being a *doran*,' Trewyn admitted. 'Angharad can do real magic, you know, though she doesn't bother very often.'

'Yes, I think Euny can too,' I said. 'I suppose that means that eventually we will do magic.'

'I used to think when I was little that it would be lovely to do magic – fancy being able to fly, or get the house to clean itself up all on its own, or have something good to eat just when you felt like it.'

'Or get to a place quickly without having to walk all the way,' I said.

'Now I'm not so sure,' said Trewyn. 'Exciting in a way, but maybe something I'd rather not meddle with. I mean, I like to feel that you can *depend* on things being predictable – apples falling downwards, a bowl of porridge being empty when it *is* empty, people being there or not being there.'

She was silent for a while and then she began to tell me of an extraordinary experience.

'I went to Caerleon on an errand for Angharad one day,' she began, 'and on the road I met a terrifying dog. It was very big – the biggest dog I had ever seen – black, with great teeth, a slavering tongue and a strange smell. It would not let me move. Every time I took a step forward it growled and looked as if it would attack me, but when I turned round and started walking slowly backwards the way I had come, the same thing happened. I stood there until noon, too frightened to move. Then it was as if I talked to Angharad inside myself, asking her what I should do. Suddenly, there she was, right beside me on the road, though she did not look at me, nor talk to me. She spoke to the dog in a language I did not understand. Then she took me by the hand and led me right past it. I looked round to see what the dog was doing and it had disappeared. But as I turned back Angharad had disappeared too.

'When I got home I asked her about it, of course. I half hoped she would deny it, say it had all been my imagination, but she simply nodded her head and said, "You needed help." Then, and this was the worst bit, she added, "That was no ordinary dog."

'"It was bigger than any dog I ever saw," I agreed.

'"I mean – it wasn't a dog at all," Angharad said. "I have a great enemy in Caerleon. I supposed he was away and that it was safe to send you. But I was mistaken. He had returned to Caerleon and he recognized you as being my apprentice."

'"How could he recognize me?" I asked. "He had never seen me."

' "Sorcerers recognize anything or anyone that belongs to a *doran* – their clothes, their animals, or their apprentices."

' "How?" I asked, and I could not believe Angharad's answer. "By their *smell*," she said.'

I was very struck by this story of Trewyn's. I was also trying to see if I could smell Trewyn, or remember whether any special smell came from Angharad. Yes, I thought, she smelled of roses. Euny's house certainly had a distinctive smell – damp and musty – and her person too had a smell – of garlic, and spice, and of unwashed skin – but I didn't smell like that. Or at least I hoped I didn't.

'Somehow,' Trewyn finished, 'that whole episode scared me. Up till then I thought magic was exciting, but then I knew that there was real danger.'

'What danger?'

'That a sorcerer could kill you, or make you his slave. They can take the spirit out of you, you know – they call it ghosting – and you wander round not knowing who you are. Sometimes now I just want to go back home and lead an ordinary life and not get mixed up in magic.'

Finally, hesitantly, I told Trewyn about the time I had done some magic myself – how I had healed Gamal. Yet, when later I had tried to cure my own chilblains, it had not worked.

'Do you think it just works when you do it for other people?' asked Trewyn. 'I mean, I've never seen Angharad use magic to make her own life easier – to save bothering to grind any more meal, say, or to avoid the labour of threading up a loom.'

*

Perhaps the talk of magic influenced me in some way. A few days before, Angharad had been showing me how to weave, and that afternoon, standing alone at the big loom while the other two were out somewhere, I had the strangest feeling that the feathery white figures I was weaving into the midnight blue background were three-dimensional, that they were just as solidly part of the world as the stool or the loom itself. Later, when I took up the spindle, I felt as if the thread was flowing not just from the puff of wool hanging over my left shoulder, but through my arm, and indeed through my whole body. For the first time the thread was perfectly even. It looked like the thread that Angharad spun, and, what was more, I knew that I was spinning somewhat as Angharad did, in an effortless rhythm.

When she came back Angharad looked at the weaving I had done and at the thread I had spun.

'So,' she said, 'you are ready!'

'Ready for what?' I asked.

'You must work hard at your cloak. Euny will be back soon.'

As so often, that day when it all seemed so easy was followed by one in which it all seemed impossibly difficult. I realized that I had made a tiny mistake in following the pattern of my weaving, but it was a long way back and I simply couldn't be bothered to undo it. In any case, the error was so tiny that it scarcely showed at all.

'What did Angharad mean, "ready"?' I asked Trewyn in our white and timber sleeping chamber. 'Ready for what?'

Trewyn's lovely face looked troubled.

'I don't know,' she said. 'Some sort of ceremony,

91

maybe. Or an ordeal – *dorans* are said to train their apprentices with ordeals.'

'What do you mean?' I asked, uneasy now myself.

'They want to find out if you are strong enough, brave enough,' she said.

'But Angharad and Euny wouldn't do anything really *cruel* to us, would they?' I asked.

'They might if they thought it would be good for us,' Trewyn replied gloomily.

I often thought about this conversation in the days that followed, as I finished the rich material of my cloak. Yet I would look across the room at Angharad's kind, motherly face, and I could not believe that she wished me any ill. And even Euny, hard as life with her had been, had never set out to hurt or frighten me – she was just not very good at imagining what I was feeling. I felt that I trusted both the *dorans*.

Trewyn, however, felt far less confident than I did. She was plainly frightened of the coming ordeal – whatever it was – and she began to sleep badly. Occasionally she would wake me with her tossing and turning. Twice she had bad dreams and began to shout in her sleep. In the morning she was pale and heavy-eyed. I saw Angharad look thoughtfully at her, and I wondered if she would give her a word of comfort, but she did not.

Angharad only spoke once about what was to come, on the day we cut the heavy material I had made from the loom. In a joyful mood that my long task was done, I picked it up and draped it for a moment around my shoulders – it was very heavy. She glanced at me, and then lowered her eyes as if she had seen more than she wanted to see.

'Take it off,' she said, quite sharply. 'It is not time.'

'When will it be time?' I enquired.

'There will be a ... ceremony,' she said. 'For you and Trewyn. When Euny returns.'

'What will it be like?'

'I cannot tell you.'

'Trewyn is very scared about it,' I said disloyally, wanting a little comfort myself.

'I know,' Angharad said, and turned to poke the fire. I was not reassured.

There was still a lot of work to be done on the cloak. From the wooden chest Angharad produced a bolt of dusky orange silk for the lining. She also gave me two topaz stones set in silver with which to make a clasp. And finally, I had to embroider a collar for it. I spent several days drawing patterns on a piece of slate, until one pattern – a design which grew unexpectedly from the look of Moon's claws – seemed exactly right to me. Angharad gave me some seed pearls to sew into the pattern, and they represented claws very convincingly.

'This will be the most precious thing you will ever own,' she said, 'and you will keep it all your life.'

On the day that I sewed the last stitch of my cloak, and Angharad folded it away for me safely in the big chest, Euny came back. It was a raw March day with a bitter east wind cutting across the moor, and Trewyn and I were glad to come home from our walk, back to the fire and a hot drink. And there was Euny, sitting on the hearth as if she had never been away.

Chapter Fourteen

The Initiation

Once or twice on my walks with Trewyn I had noticed an oddly shaped building near to the circle of standing stones where she often liked to go and sit. It was made of stone and the walls curved upwards to make a straight ridge. The line of the ridge, I had noticed once, pointed to the centre of the stone circle. One day, when the rain was pelting down, we had pushed open the creaking wooden door and gone inside. It was much bigger than appeared from the outside, with a plain earth floor, which looked as if it had been recently raked and a centre hearth with a fire already laid upon it. We could only see this by leaving the door open since there were no slits or holes in the walls to give light.

'Someone uses this place,' I remarked to Trewyn. 'But who? And for what?' She made some reply about it being a shepherd's hut, but I knew what they looked like – tiny, rudely-constructed, wooden buildings, with just room for a man to curl up and sleep out of the wind and the rain. Not like this, at all.

Back at home I noticed that Angharad was no longer pushing us to continual spinning and weaving – she gave us time to idle the day away as she had never done before. She and Euny were often deep in conversation – not always agreeing, I suspect – the sort of conversation that breaks off as soon as you come into the room.

'Something funny's going on,' I said to Trewyn.

'It's the ceremony,' she replied anxiously. 'They are getting us ready for it.'

One April afternoon they called us in – we had been punting on the lake on a raft we had laboriously nailed together. Trewyn had pond-weed clinging round one leg, from pushing the raft out with me on it, and her clothes were wringing wet. I was scarcely looking better. I had torn my smock and my hair was wild and knotted from blowing in the wind. We were a dreadful sight.

'You must both be bathed,' Angharad said (and I could see enormous cauldrons of water already steaming on the fire). 'Wash every part of yourselves, including your hair.'

As we took it in turns to use the tub, and to wash one another's backs, Trewyn said to me in a quiet voice, 'It's going to happen.' I could feel her hands trembling. Certainly there did seem to be something odd going on. When we got out of the tub we were given a big cloth each on which to dry ourselves. There was no sign of clean clothes.

'Shall I go up and get a clean smock?' I asked at last.

Instead of replying Angharad simply handed me a huge sheet, and she gave another to Trewyn.

We were combing out our long wet hair in front of the fire when I said, 'Is supper going to be soon?'

'You are fasting,' said Euny.

'We are all fasting,' Angharad amended.

Trewyn and I exchanged nervous glances.

'Why?' Trewyn finally croaked out.

Angharad shook her head as if she could not answer and Euny looked out of the door as she had done several times already. It was dark, and a wind was blowing, whining ominously around Angharad's house. I wished that if something frightening had to happen to us it could happen on some other night, or better yet, by day. Trewyn and I had already speculated on every possibility – would they beat us or torture us? Make us eat or drink horrible substances? Both of us were sure that we had heard stories of such things. We sat on by the fire, two substantial ghosts, and after a bit the full moon, huge and brilliant, appeared in the sky. Euny nodded to Angharad. 'Time to go,' she said.

They stood up, taking the sheets from us, and said, 'We are going out.'

'Where are our clothes?' asked Trewyn, her slim body tense with her distress.

'No clothes,' said Angharad. 'You will go just like that.'

'I can't,' Trewyn wailed. 'We might meet someone.'

'We won't meet anyone,' said Euny definitely. 'Come along. There is work to be done.'

Trewyn threw an agonized glance in my direction, hoping, perhaps, that I would join her in a rebellion. For some reason I was less fearful than she. I simply followed Angharad and Euny to the door. Once outside the stones hurt my feet, the wind, which was cold, blew painfully on my bare flesh, and quite soon my teeth were chattering. Even the soft tickle of my loose hair on my bare shoulders felt unfamiliar. What were we doing? And why? The moon, a huge yellow disk at the end of the path we were following, lit the landscape in precise lines without shadow. Trewyn's trembling naked body in front of me shone in a gold light.

Only when we reached the stone hut did I realize that that was where we were heading. It was a relief to march our cold bodies out of the bitter wind, though the only place on which to sit was a cold stone. There was a fire laid on the centre hearth and two big piles of wood beside it. I looked wistfully at the unlit fire, my body shaking and shuddering with cold.

The four of us sat down and Angharad and Euny lit a rush lamp and began reciting, by heart, a long and very tedious poem. It spoke of dead heroes and heroines, most of whom I had never heard of; it was a recital of the interminable history of the *dorans*, whose wisdom had been frequently persecuted. At the end the words began to be addressed to me and Trewyn, admonitions that we should be worthy of our high calling, should enter into harmony with the world, should care for others, should never work magic for our own aggrandizement.

Then Euny bade us lie face downward full-length upon the ground.

'Think before you answer these questions,' she told us. 'Do you wish to be admitted to the order of *doran*?' she wanted to know.

Lying shivering on the cold ground I wished that I was safely home in bed. If this was what being a *doran* was all about it was hard to see why anyone should wish to be one. Yet when I thought of the hazel tree, of the strange way that Euny and I had come together, and of my experiences at Angharad's house as I wove the cloth for my cloak, I knew that life was pushing me towards the particular sort of wisdom that Euny and Angharad had. I felt that I had no real choice.

'I wish to become a *doran*,' I said through my chattering teeth.

I waited for Trewyn to make a similar declaration, but she lay in silence.

'Trewyn?' Angharad asked at length.

'I don't know,' Trewyn wailed. 'I'm frightened.'

I could hear Angharad and Euny conferring.

'Very well,' Angharad said at last. 'We will continue with the ritual. At the end of it, Trewyn, we will ask you the question again and if then you answer no, you will leave us and never mention to anyone what you have seen here.'

One of them had touched a light to the fire on the hearth and I could hear twigs crackling.

'You may get up and come to the fire,' Euny said to us and we sat on our haunches beside it. Trewyn was weeping, whereas I felt a kind of sullen anger.

Euny took a handful of herbs from a bowl on the ground and began to chew them. Then she passed the bowl to Angharad, who followed her example.

I was surprised to see Euny now piling green wood on the fire, when there was a perfectly good supply of dry wood. In a few minutes, inevitably, the stone hut was filled with acrid smoke. My eyes brimmed with tears, I began to cough convulsively, and for a few moments I lost sight of the others in the smoke. Feeling that I was suffocating I made for the wooden door, but found that I could not open it. To my surprise, it appeared to be bolted on the outside.

Groping my way back in the smoke I bumped into Trewyn and we sat with our arms round one another, still shaking with cold, as far from the fire as we could get. Then the smoke cleared a little, and to our astonishment Angharad and Euny had disappeared!

I noticed that the green wood had been placed in a separate pile and I had no doubt that the two *dorans* had deliberately filled the hut with smoke. But there was another huge pile of dry wood next to it and I put two large logs on the fire. Trewyn crept back to the hearth, still coughing.

'Why did they do it?' she asked. 'Is it part of the test?'

I was so angry at being locked into the hut that I could scarcely speak.

'You do suppose they intend to come back?' asked Trewyn tremulously. 'They wouldn't just leave us here?'

'Of course they'll come back,' I said, with a confidence that was not entirely real. Suppose the two of us were destined to be some sort of sacrifice? Suppose they were going to leave us to starve?

Just at that moment my eye fell on a plate of sweetmeats that I had seen Angharad preparing earlier in the day. I did not know she had brought them with her, but I was both hungry and angry and I decided that, whatever Angharad might say about it, I would stave off my hunger pangs with the honey sweets.

'Here,' I said to Trewyn. She hastily took a piece, then asked, 'Won't they mind?'

'They should have thought of that before they left them behind,' I replied. The sweets were delicious.

I noticed a shabby wooden chest in the far corner of the hut, and dragged it closer to the fire. For a few minutes Trewyn and I sat on it – it was warmer than the cold stones – then slid down on to the earth floor and sat leaning against one another, propped up by the chest, our feet comfortably toasting by the fire.

'Do you *see* anything?' Trewyn asked hesitantly after a while.

'No. But I feel a lot warmer.'

Even as I spoke, though, I noticed the grain in the wooden door, as the firelight flickered over it. It looked like the markings on a snake's back, and, like a snake, it moved. I did not feel threatened, simply delighted at the beauty of the design.

'The door!' I said to Trewyn.

'Snakes!' she said cheerfully, and I felt full of love for her that she could share this vision with me. I continued to nibble the sweets and to pass them to Trewyn, and now I noticed that the stones on the walls shone with a sort of golden light. The shadows between them were deep and lustrous, and there were faces – not ugly or frightening faces as sometimes in dreams, but very ancient faces, some sideways ones with hooked noses, some with gentle and closed eyes. Tracing out these faces fascinated me so much that I was silent for a long time.

The fire was another source of wonder. Gazing into its shifting and hissing depths I saw an extraordinary sight. There was a branch with buds of apple blossom upon it, probably culled from one of Angharad's old trees. As I watched, the warmth caused the buds to open. For a moment I gazed at the perfect flowers until the flames caught them too and quickly reduced the whole branch to ashes. I felt that Trewyn and I were like the buds coming into flower in our youth and beauty, one day achieving our moment of perfection, then returning to the nothingness from which we came.

'Are you still frightened?' I asked her.

'Oh no, not at all. Well, not of being a *doran*. It's what we have to be, isn't it? You and me. It's what we're meant for, don't you think?'

Chapter Fifteen

The Ceremony

Warm from the heat of the fire, busy in the caverns and passages of our own minds, Trewyn and I dozed, propped up against the wooden chest. When I at last awoke, Angharad and Euny were sitting once more on the far side of the fire, looking as if they had never disappeared. They sat still and silent, without a glance in our direction.

They were different, however, as everything else was different. Both of them had the same golden glow that I had noticed in the stones. The fold of the yellow shawl that Angharad wore seemed deep with mystery. Even Euny's worn black garments had a luminous sheen to them. Angharad's face, always full of kindness, now seemed so pure, generous and good that I felt full of reverence, as I looked at it. Euny's dark, stern face held the desperate sadness of a lost little girl, yet I could see how gradually, painfully, that loneliness had grown into a great strength. Euny, I saw (though I felt I had always known this about her), was totally without fear. Whatever this strange uncomfortable ceremony was about, I decided Angharad and Euny were to be trusted.

Euny was now building up the fire, though it was already hot in the hut, and Angharad had begun to chant a slow rhythmic melody. Trewyn and I had been taught the words and automatically we joined in. As the heat grew in the hut I could feel the perspiration running down my face. Trewyn too looked desperately hot and turned anguished eyes to me. Yet Euny was still pushing twigs and logs into the fire.

Angharad and Euny now rose to their feet, and with Angharad making the mouth music I had often heard her make at her loom, they began a sort of dance. It was nothing like the kind of merry occasion in which young men and women dance together. Rather it was as if Euny and Angharad were tracing out a pattern upon the floor, seeking some knowledge with their feet. Occasionally they touched hands, turned towards, or away from, each other, led by the strange crooning cry of Angharad's singing, weaving the shape of the dance. First Trewyn, then I, got up and found ourselves irresistibly dancing with them with sure steps that no-one had ever taught us. We danced, it seemed to me, for hours, weaving and dipping, turning and touching hands. Sometimes we danced – sometimes the dance danced us.

I think after this we all slept in total exhaustion. I was aware of waking once, cold, since the fire had died down, stiff from the iron hardness of the ground, and desperately hungry. I could see daylight under the door, and I longed briefly to be part of that world outside, but sleep mercifully drew me back again into its embrace.

Much later, Trewyn was shaking me.
'Wake up! Look, the door's open!'
With an enormous effort I threw off the web of sleep. I could smell sweet fresh air through

the open door – though both Trewyn and I were shivering with cold. We could see the dark sky with a few stars twinkling in it. There was no sign of Angharad or Euny.

'What do we do now?' I asked.

Without further conversation we left the hut with its dead embers. High up on the hill by the standing stones we caught sight of a bonfire and we moved towards it. Cold and dishevelled, wondering what fresh ordeals awaited us, we stumbled into the ring of standing stones and then stopped in astonishment. Angharad and Euny stood by the fire, as if waiting. Angharad wore a shining brown cloak clasped with yellow stones and Euny wore a cloak figured in green and yellow and black. They signalled to us to join them by the fire. Each had a bundle at her feet and I was surprised to recognize the cloak I had so laboriously woven lying on the ground beside Euny. She came to me with a soft white tunic. She lifted it over my head and the folds fell to my feet. She fastened it at the neck, tied a girdle around my waist, then took a comb made of bone and combed the earth and the tangles from my hair. She placed a pair of deerskin slippers upon my feet, then lifted the heavy cloak and, easing it about my shoulders, joined the topaz clasp. It was lovely to feel the cloak's warmth and weight.

Meanwhile Angharad had also dressed Trewyn. When all was done, they embraced both of us, and Trewyn, in her warm, affectionate way, turned and hugged me. I could see in her eyes the thought that now we were really sisters.

Angharad took a loaf of wheaten bread and broke it in her strong fingers. She handed each of us a piece, and I ate mine eagerly. Even in my hungriest days with Euny food had never tasted as good as this. I could smell the wheat and the yeast in it, taste the salt. Then Angharad passed us a big cup of wine, and each of us took a long draught. There was a spicy taste to it and I guessed she had added some secret herb. Just then, white and ghostlike in the starlight, I saw great wings floating above me, and there, big and silent, was Moon.

Chapter Sixteen

Defying Euny

Next morning, when we woke up in Angharad's house, Trewyn and I made an odd discovery. 'Watch this,' she said to me, 'I've just discovered it.'

There was a moment's pause and then her smock, which was lying over a chair got up – that is the only word for it – and moved across the room and flopped down on the floor. There was another pause, during which I could feel her concentrating hard and then it rose up again and returned to the place it had come from.

I was impressed and at once determined to outdo her. A candle stood on the table, the one that had lighted us to bed the night before. I closed my eyes, concentrated, thinking only of the candle. When I opened them again the candle was alight! Trewyn then put the candle out without moving from her bed, I lit it again and she put it out.

'I know,' said Trewyn, 'let's see if we can make something. Both of us together.' We agreed on a spider and almost at once a spider ran across the floor.

In the days that followed we both had a passion for trying out our new skills. We hid this from Angharad and Euny, sensing that they would think us very frivolous, but we simply could not stop. As soon as we were alone together, or out for a walk, we would start on our trumpery magic. It was the greatest fun and difficult to believe that we would ever tire of it. I am sure that Angharad at least, hearing the shouts of laughter that came from our room, knew very well what we were up to, but she never said a word. Perhaps she reflected that our time together was coming to an end.

We had changed in another way too since the day of the ceremony.

'Do you notice something different about your sense of smell?' I asked Trewyn tentatively one day. She nodded.

'I can smell you and Angharad and Euny – not just the usual human smells, but *something else*. It's as if they tell me something, just as the expression on a person's face tells you something about them. I can smell Angharad's goodness and Euny's strength. I can smell your healing wisdom.'

'And I can smell your beauty!'

We asked Angharad about it and she confirmed, as if surprised that we should even ask, that smell was one of the skills of a *doran*.

It was early summer when Euny and I set off home, and our journey this time was pleasant. The hedgerows were fragrant with roses and honeysuckle, the meadow-sweet billowed beneath them, the sky was a wide, cloudless blue, and we heard the cuckoo sing its late song. As we crossed the meadows, skylarks, high above us, rinsed our ears with their joyful din. We walked along the edges of cornfields full of young

grain, past gardens from which we helped ourselves to tender pea pods, through misty blue
woods, through dim forests and over gentle hills.
Sometimes, far away, we could see the glimmer
of the sea. This time we slept warmly at
nights, full of Angharad's oatcake and fermented
whey. One evening, as we ate our supper, Euny
surprised me.

'Angharad said I did not feed you properly.
Because I eat little I forget that young things
need their food. I'll try to do better.'

Euny said this without embarrassment or
shame, but just as a fact. Angharad had pointed
it out to her, and now she understood. I was
touched.

'It's all right,' I said awkwardly.

I had felt very sad at leaving Trewyn and
Angharad, not to mention the comfort of Angharad's
house, but I found that I took pleasure in being
alone again with Euny, that although no word
of affection was expressed and there were no em-
braces, her austere warmth towards me glad-
dened and pleased me. Since the time in the stone
hut she seemed a little more friendly, as if she
was sure of me in some way. The long days in
the open air, the nights of sound sleep, made
me feel extraordinarily well.

As we came out of the forest near Euny's hut, and
I saw the great shadow of the tor above us I felt
a little shiver of excitement and joy. It was not
dark, but already a brilliant silver moon hung
in the sky over the tor. Rain had made a pool
on the grass in front of the hill and sitting upon
it were twelve swans, their beautiful heads and
wings mirrored in the water. The sun shone upon

the tor at an angle that lit it strangely. Its bare, terraced sides were shadowed, its outline haloed. Euny and I stood quite still and Euny made some exclamation under her breath – it might have been an incantation or a prayer.

After a few moments she walked on, and I followed. The hut, with its dead embers, some mouldering pig hanging on a hook from the ceiling, its threadbare rug and pathetic bits of furniture, seemed unwelcoming, dusty and cold, and for a moment my heart sank. Bearing the dreadful meat outside under Euny's orders, however, I saw the moon through the branches of the hazel tree, and the outline of the hill springing behind it, and I knew that this was the place where I should be.

Euny had seated herself with unusual weariness in her old rocking-chair, and it was I who lit a fire, who swept and dusted, who made soup with the remains of the vegetables that Angharad had given us. Going outside to gather herbs I saw the empty pigsty and remembered the incident before we had left home.

After supper I counted on my fingers. 'Three months before I go back to my father,' I said. Euny nodded.

'There is a lot to do,' she said. As always with Euny, I could not bring myself to ask *what* there was to do, and she never explained.

Within a few days Euny and I had fallen straight back into our old routines. There were the household chores, the long silences, the meagre meals. But Angharad's words had driven her to try harder to feed me. On the day after we returned home she disappeared without a word and came back several hours later, laden with a large sack of wheaten flour. I immediately started making bread and cakes with it, as Angharad had taught me. On other days she returned with eggs and honey and cabbages, and a set of newly-hatched little chicks which she gave to me to rear. I was enchanted by their furry little bodies and loved to pick them up in my hands. When one or two of them died, as such chicks do, I grieved over them, to Euny's irritation.

It seems to me now that I needed someone, something to love. I missed Angharad and Trewyn badly. Though she noticed every flower and berry and cloud, and every turn of the wind, it felt as if Euny could only live with *me* by forgetting and ignoring me for much of the time.

Angharad had given me some material to make a palliasse for myself, and when I stuffed the bag with straw I found that I lay much more comfortably and warmly at nights. She had also made me a blanket, in a brilliant pattern of dusky orange and midnight blue. I was never cold beneath it and it hung over the back of the rocking-chair by day, giving the room a vivid focus. I picked flowers too, taking one of our few bowls to set them in.

I was out in the meadow near the hut one day picking some wild lilies when I heard the sound of hoofs on the track. And there was my beloved Gamal! I was so thrilled to see him that it took me a few moments to notice that there was another rider behind him. To my dismay it was Finbar. Gamal gave a whoop of pleasure at seeing me, shouted to Finbar, and came across the field. Then Gamal and I began to talk.

He wanted to know where I had been – he had come several times in search of me. I wanted to hear about everyone at Castle Dore. He had brought me a present from Meroot – some wind-dried meat that was a special delicacy among our people. Finbar listened patiently, smiling. Since their last visit, I had considered Finbar as a sort of enemy, but he seemed to be perfectly friendly towards me. It was disconcerting.

'We thought we could stay here overnight and then spend tomorrow together,' said Gamal. My heart sank slightly. How would I persuade Euny to let me have the day to myself?

'I'll go and ask Euny,' I said nervously.

Euny was sitting rocking herself placidly in the hut, and in the way that was typical of her she knew what I had come to ask before I asked it.

'They needn't think I'm going to feed them,' she said.

'Couldn't we?' I pleaded. 'We've plenty of meal.'

Euny did not answer.

'I could make some porridge or something . . .'

'And you can't have time off to play with them. We have a lot of work to do.'

I felt furious both at her lack of hospitality and her unfairness. I went out slamming the hut door behind me.

Gamal noticed my crestfallen expression at once.

'It's all right,' he said. 'We can sleep out in the meadow in our blankets.'

'She won't give you any food,' I said. I had grown up in a tradition that treated the guest as sacred, and I felt humiliated.

'We've got enough in our saddle-bags.'

111

'But I *will* come out with you tomorrow. I'll pretend to be going to the well to get water and then I'll run off with you.'

Finbar, I could see, admired me for this but Gamal looked a bit worried.

'Won't you get into awful trouble?' he asked.

I shrugged. The thought of a day's fun was worth it.

The next morning I set off with my buckets, left them lying by the well, and ran off with Gamal and Finbar. We rode to a distant beach, splashed in the sea for hours, climbed rocks and sunned ourselves. Gamal played to us on his flute. Then I rode Gamal's pony along the sand and it was wonderful to feel the motion of a horse beneath me.

'You do ride well,' Finbar said admiringly, and my heart slightly softened towards him, though I gave no indication of this. Also, when he caught a fish he came and presented it to me as if giving me a present. But I scarcely acknowledged it. I could not forget the shame of the occasion when I had killed the pig, the mockery in Finbar's eyes at a moment when I was so unhappy. In any case, I wanted Gamal to myself. As if sensing my wish to be alone with Gamal, Finbar went off for a long ride by himself.

'How's Meroot?' I asked Gamal. A shadow passed across his face and he shrugged without replying. What he wanted to talk about was music. A new musician had come to court since I had left and was secretly teaching Gamal.

'It's not so much playing that interests me now. I have started to make up music. Evert sang a song I had composed one night at dinner and Meroot said how beautiful it was – without knowing it was mine, of course.'

'She would never let you be a musician, would she?'

'No-one can stop me thinking of music – not even Meroot,' said Gamal.

As the afternoon wore on I grew a bit fearful of going back to confront Euny.

'Do you want us to come with you?' Gamal asked.

'No, go on home,' I said. Gamal promised to come again, but I felt very sad as they cantered off along the beach.

I noticed as I passed the well that the buckets were still lying there, so I filled them and took them back with me. Euny was sitting in the rocking-chair, as if she had spent the whole day there. I braced myself for a scolding, but none came. In fact, I had an odd sort of feeling that she was rather pleased with me. I could not understand it at all. In fact, it was quite disturbing.

Chapter Seventeen

My Return

Next day Euny suddenly started to instruct me in the way I had longed for at the beginning, sitting me down and giving me long hours of teaching about spells, herbs, good magic and bad magic. First, she made me give demonstrations of the sort of skills Trewyn and I had practised – making things move, appear and disappear – then told me sternly that that was quite enough and that she hoped I would never waste my energies with that kind of thing again.

'Different *dorans* have different gifts,' she said. 'Yours will be to do with healing people, which is partly about a special kind of knowing and partly about a long and difficult study of herbs.'

I was surprised that Euny knew that I had healing gifts; I had always felt shy about telling her.

'Oh, I knew because of the white owl,' she said, annoyed at being interrupted. 'It was perfectly obvious. All those under the protection of the owl know about healing.'

'What is the special kind of knowing?' I asked her.

'Being able to pay attention to people. Not just with your mind, but with every part of you. Then you see the sickness quite clearly. I cannot help you with that. What I can teach you, before you go home, is the lore of herbs. As well as some other healing skills.'

Euny had, of course, taught me to recognize many herbs in my first weeks with her. Now the task was to learn their uses by heart, to discover how to combine them, how to make them into pills and ointments, decoctions, tinctures and teas.

She taught me to make clearwater, the colour-less liquid that protects a *doran* against sorcery, steeping rowan and other herbs in water where gold has lain. She explained to me about the terrible curses used by sorcerers which bring slow and miserable death upon those who are their victims, and then recounted some of the rituals great *dorans* have used to dissolve curses.

'There is no one way of doing it — you just have to use your wits and your imagination — but remember that earth, air, fire and water are your allies . . .'

She taught me what to do for someone who has had a 'sad' spell laid on them by a sorcerer, or the kind of spell that makes all places and people strike deadly fear. Even more important, she said, was to know what to do for a person who was 'ghosted' — that is, captured and enslaved by a sorcerer in such a way that they no longer had a will or mind of their own.

The spells and recipes she taught me were long and complicated. The only way to be sure of them was to learn them by heart and then to repeat them to her time after time, which she made me do endlessly until she was quite sure I had mastered them. She would not permit me to change even unimportant words, but insisted that I repeat the words she used, even, it seemed to me, in her actual tone of voice. I was so interested in what she was teaching me that I found this laborious learning quite pleasurable.

Now the weeks passed very quickly. Once or twice Gamal came again, this time alone.

'Tell me truly about Meroot,' I said, remembering his reluctance to speak of her. 'Is something wrong with her? Is she ill?'

'Not as you mean it. Only, I think there *is* something wrong with her.'

'Can you explain?'

'I will tell you what I think. It is that she still dreams that one day, when your father is dead, I will take over his kingdom.'

Embarrassed, Gamal looked away from me, out over the countryside.

'Would you want to do that?' I asked, my voice wobbling at the thought of my father dead.

'That is not the point. Last birthday I swore my allegiance to the king. Plotting against him is against the rule of the knights.'

I was silent, not knowing what to say.

'There is something else.' Gamal's voice cracked, with shame and anguish. 'You know that Meroot can do magic, is . . . perhaps . . . a sorceress. I'm afraid what she might do.'

I shivered with fear of Meroot, but put out a hand and patted Gamal's hand.

'I will be back home soon,' I said, 'then we may talk more of these things. Perhaps I could warn my father.' Gamal shook his head gloomily, as if in doubt that we could save the situation.

That night I told Euny about the conversation, and she listened with her head on one side like a bird.

'Your magic is at least as strong as Meroot's magic,' she said. 'You have been well taught.

There is perhaps only one other who may be stronger.'

'Who is the other?'

'There is a wizard in Wales.'

'Angharad's old enemy!'

I shivered at the dangers hidden in her words.

'I must try to oppose Meroot then?'

Euny spoke drily.

'Perhaps it was for this that you were born.'

The relationship between Euny and me had suddenly become quite different. Instead of treating me as her servant, Euny now did her full share of the household chores – fetching water from the well, cleaning out the fire, preparing meals, sweeping and tidying. There was a note of respect, of listening to what I said, which I did not remember before. For the first time since I had come to live with her there was a sense of peace, of pleasantness and ease, which reminded me of the life of Angharad and Trewyn.

As, day by day, Euny imparted her secrets to me, I knew that the seasons were wheeling to the place when I must soon again return to my father, though I knew, too, that at some time in the future I would return to Euny for the rituals that would complete my training as a *doran*.

'What will happen when I go back home?' I asked Euny. 'Must I marry?'

'Do you want to marry?' she asked.

'I don't know. Not yet, anyway. I'm only a child.'

'Who will rule the kingdom when your father dies?' Euny asked sharply. 'Will it be you?'

I shrugged. 'Because women are not warriors it is difficult for them to rule.'

'I don't see why,' said Euny. 'There are other

117

important things in kingship besides warfare.'

'I'm not sure if I could rule,' I said uncertainly. 'What difference will being a *doran* make? I thought that was a vocation of its own.'

'You will have to see,' said Euny unhelpfully.

'Will you miss me when I am gone?' I rashly asked her.

Euny tossed her head in a gesture I knew well. 'I need nobody,' she said. 'Certainly not you.'

I was not as crushed as I would formerly have been.

'Well, I shall miss you,' I said, 'and I believe that you will miss me.' I could see by the obstinate gleam in her eye that she had no intention of giving me the satisfaction of telling me she cared for me.

On the day of my departure for Castle Dore she watched me as I lifted Moon gently down from his perch and put him into his travelling bag.

'I am coming with you to help you carry your things,' Euny said suddenly. Since I had nothing but my *doran's* cloak, a dress and a shawl or two, Angharad's blanket, and a little food and water for the journey, that was scarcely necessary, and I knew she was merely using it as an excuse.

'I shall miss the hut,' I said, looking round it for the last time.

'It will still be here,' Euny said pettishly. 'You can come and see it when you can spare the time from your grand life.'

I wept a little as we walked through the forest. I felt as if nothing would console me for the loss of those hard days which, I now realized, had taught me a great deal. I would not see the tor, nor the hazel tree, when I woke up each morning. I would not see Euny.

When Castle Dore appeared in the distance Euny stopped. She put her hands into the folds of her gown and brought out two large flasks and some other objects and laid them on the ground in front of her.

'Here are your "protections",' she told me, using the *doran* word. 'If there is the slightest chance of your running into danger you must carry them with you at all times.'

One of the protections was a crescent moon on a leather string, and Euny put it over my head with the air of investing me with an honour. The next thing she gave me was a black egg.

'If you are in danger of your life you may break this egg,' she said. 'But be careful. If you do it when the danger is not severe you will be unprotected when the real danger comes. As come it will, early or late. So use it wisely.'

'But how will I *know*?' I said in a sort of wail, already certain that I would break the egg at the wrong moment. Euny gave me a withering look and did not deign to answer.

'Clearwater you know about,' she added giving me the two flasks. 'After this you must make your own.'

I tucked all the protections away into my bundle and then looked up to speak to Euny and she was gone! The long straight track was quite empty, only it seemed to me that I could hear her cackle of laughter echoing in the air.

I walked on soberly. I was nervous about my return. As I approached Castle Dore I was surprised to see a great flock of rooks wheeling about the place. I had never seen rooks there before and their black wings and persistent cries gave an air of menace.

The guards saluted when I reached the entrance – I found my way quickly through the trick of the maze and into the big enclosure of the castle. The doors of the hall and the council chamber stood wide so that I knew my father must be within his own chambers. I went straight to my parents' apartment and found my mother reading, and my father writing on his tablet. The glimpse I caught of him through the lattice before he saw me suggested that he was worried – he looked older, bent with care.

I stood in the doorway.

'I have come back.'

My mother and my father embraced me and made me feel that after all I was glad to be back at the Wooden Palace.

'Tell me,' said the king, 'did Euny teach you all that you hoped.'

'It was very hard,' I told him. 'But I learned more, much more than I knew there was to learn.'

'And you have come back here to marry?'

'I don't know,' I said. 'Do you wish me to marry?'

He hesitated, exchanging glances with my mother, as if weighing up different ideas in his mind, then said, 'We will talk of this later. Tonight we will have a feast for your return. See that you wear a fine gown – not that rag you have on your back – and that your hair is dressed with jewels.'

I bowed before him because, after all, he was the king, and I went to my old apartment.

It was strange to be back in the comforts of Castle Dore. Although my own chamber was cold and empty, Erith soon bustled in, embraced me with joy, and lit a fire. While I waited she had a servant bring me a plate of chicken and some white bread, both of which I ate hungrily. She summoned other servants who brought water heated in the kitchen. As she had so often done in the past she bathed me – exclaiming in horror at the callouses on my hands and the blisters on my feet and observing how thin I was – then she dressed me in a yellow silk gown which went well with my dark hair. She found a fillet of silver and bound my hair with it, placed a torque of silver round my neck, and bracelets upon my arms. When I looked at myself in the big bronze mirror I saw how grown-up I had become – very different from the child who had last sought her reflection there. I was slender and pretty, I thought with youthful pride, and the heat of the fire had brought a pleasing pink to my cheeks. When I went to join my father I held my head high. King Mark's daughter had come home.

My father was expecting me and gave me a long appreciative look and a smile. He was obviously pleased. Together we walked to the Great Hall where his knights waited to dine with him, and together we walked through the big room while the pipes and drums played for us. I sat beside his carved chair in my smaller one, and when he took up his knife he cut a piece of the roast swan and presented it to me – the custom used by my people to make a guest welcome.

The evening proceeded as I remembered many evenings doing in the past – the slow meal that I had always found so tedious once my appetite was satisfied. There were a number of courses, but, was it my imagination? There seemed less food than there had been in the past. While we ate a bard sang a song of love and adventure.

Perhaps because I had lived such a simple life with Euny, because I was genuinely hungry, or because my recent experiences had made me look at the world with a fresh eye, everything tonight seemed wonderfully interesting. I enjoyed the faces of the knights – some of them old and scarred with battle, others still in the pride of young manhood. I savoured the bright colours of the clothes and jewels, the harmonies of the music, the glorious taste and smell of the food, the rich scent and ruby tint of the wine, the beauty and intelligence of the dogs which crouched beside my father. I leaned across and laid my hand upon my father's.

'It's good to be back,' I told him.

Afterwards, as we sat near the fire, the knights came up and talked to me – men who had nursed me as a child. The young squires, no older than I was myself, who had sat at the lowest table, eyed me shyly, one or two of them looking as if they would like to talk. I went about the room, enjoying the lively company and the handsome young men. Yet . . . many of them had a pallor, a kind of weariness about them, that puzzled me. Surely they had not always been like that?

Even after my father had left the hall I stayed, talking and laughing. At one moment my eyes strayed towards the door. Two tall boys were leaving and one of them was half-turned, laughing, to catch a comment the other had made. It was, of course, Gamal and Finbar, both grown so tall. Gamal waved, Finbar bowed, with just the faintest suggestion of friendly mockery. I grinned back at them.

Later, in my parents' apartment, I sat on a footstool between them as I had often done as a child. In reply to their questions I told them a little more of my life with Euny, and asked them about life at Castle Dore.

But I could see a shadow in my mother's face and my father moved like an old man in his chair. He was very thin, I noticed.

'There is trouble?' I asked him, expecting a story of raids and plundering, of the need to lead his young men to some horrific battle from which many would not return. He clasped and unclasped his hands in a wretchedness I had not seen before. He was not a fearful man, and had always had a certain appetite for the excitement of war, though he grieved at the human cost.

A look of shame and pain crossed his face.

'The crops have done badly,' said my mother. 'Many animals have died for no reason that we can discover.'

'Is it magic?' I asked.

'There have always been years when the crops failed,' said my father crossly, 'and years when the animals have been sick.'

'Not often both together,' said my mother, and I could see that she, too, suspected magic.

'Do you suspect anyone?' I said to her. She did not answer, but again exchanged a glance with my father, and I guessed that they had had many conversations on this subject.

'We cannot speak of it tonight,' she said. 'It is too late. Come and see us tomorrow and I will say more.'

Chapter Eighteen

Meroot's Curse

The next morning there was a light tap on my door at dawn. Accustomed to early rising, I was already awake. I opened it quietly, not to disturb Erith, and found Gamal waiting outside.

'Come out for a ride!' he whispered. In a few minutes I was dressed. He had two horses saddled and ready, and soon we were miles away on a hillside overlooking the sea. We breakfasted out of the wind in a hollow – Gamal had thoughtfully brought bread and some cold meat.

'Is it good to be back?' he asked me.

I hesitated.

'It is lovely to be home, but . . . my father seems ill, and the harvest was so bad that he fears famine,' I said.

Gamal nodded. He looked miserable, I thought.

'Something is very wrong,' I added. He was silent, but I felt that there was more that he could have said if he had chosen to do so. Then he mentioned a piece of court news that I had already heard – that Meroot intended to marry again.

'A knight from Caerleon,' he said. I was aware that the name stirred some troubling memory in me, though I could not think what it was.

'She will marry in December,' said Gamal shortly. 'The king is to give a great feast for her.'

*

As we returned home I noticed a sort of bleakness about the countryside that I did not remember from previous winters. The sheep looked sickly and listless, and the people grey and afraid. Even at Castle Dore, now that I was no longer excited to be back, I saw that everyone looked pale, tired and dispirited.

The next day I called upon Meroot as etiquette dictated, to greet her upon my return and to congratulate her upon her marriage. She received me in the little house my father had built for her – she had never ceased to complain about its smallness – and we drank a sweet tawny wine from across the sea and ate honey biscuits. The room was very bare, save for an odd-looking leather stick that stood propped again the wall. Meroot wore a grey dress, with a turquoise and silver collar; her wrists were heavy with jewellery of jet and silver. She was accompanied by a huge black hound that I had never seen before, collared, like her, in turquoise and silver. It was so big that I could not take my eyes off it. A pastille burned in a dish giving the room a scent of lilies, yet somewhere beneath that scent there were other smells, sharp and sour and sickening.

'So what did Euny teach you?' Meroot wished to know. Though it was the same question that my father had asked, the way it was asked was quite different.

'She taught me healing arts,' I said carefully. 'She taught me the dose for sicknesses, and the way of touching to make people well. And Angharad of the West taught me to spin and to weave.'

'Angharad!' she said, in obvious surprise.

'Do you know her?'

'I did once.'

The silence fell heavily between us until Meroot left the room to fetch more wine. She closed the door behind her and I glanced around the room. The leather stick caught my eye again and I stood up and moved towards it. Immediately the black hound growled softly in its throat and moved between me and the stick. I sat down uneasily. Suddenly I had the oddest feeling that I was being watched, that through a knot in the door, or a hole in the tapestry, Meroot's cold blue eye was fixed upon me. I composed myself as unselfconsciously as possible and wondered why she should do such a thing. What could she see that she could not observe when she sat in front of me?

At that moment the outer door opened and Gamal came in, hot and weary, wearing parts of his armour and carrying the rest over his arm. He smiled when he saw me, and sat down, filthy as he was from the practice field. It seemed to me that once again I heard the dog growl softly in its throat, though it did not move. But then Meroot came back, the dog slunk back to its corner, and Gamal and I fell silent. I was glad when I could go home without appearing rude.

My mother was alone that afternoon when I called upon my parents.

'It's Meroot, isn't it?' I said without delay. 'You are afraid she is laying a curse upon Castle Dore?'

Erlain nodded.

'Your father won't hear of it. He is loyal to her, and it is destroying the kingdom.' Erlain's eyes filled with tears. 'I was wondering, Ninnoc. Do you know any magic that might help us?'

My first thought was to send for Euny, but then I remembered that she had gone away on a visit to Angharad. I felt both excited and frightened. I had not dreamed that I might need to use my new skills so soon. 'Let me think about it,' I said. Before I left Erlain I gave her a phial of Euny's clearwater and told her how to anoint herself with it.

'See if you can persuade father to use it too,' I said, not very hopefully. Lying in bed I thought about the careful schooling I had had in magic — how I had learned all that my wise teacher could tell me. Now I should find out if my education was equal to the challenge. Just as I was falling asleep I remembered, with a start that woke me right up again, that it was at Caerleon that Trewyn had encountered a sorcerer and been saved by Angharad. Suppose, just suppose, I thought, that Meroot's new husband was the great sorcerer. This would mean that he was also the sinister enemy of Angharad whom Trewyn had once described to me. Was this why Meroot was startled to hear Angharad's name? If she had not known it before, Meroot now knew that Angharad and Euny were friends.

Already the plans were going forward for Meroot's wedding. Wines were being taken from our cellars, pigs, chickens, and swans were being fattened, and deer were being hunted. Soon we should start making pies, baking and roasting.

Gifts for the bride from the Grey Knight of Caerleon began to arrive; silks and spices, scent and rare fruits, inlaid boxes containing jewels, nightingales in cages, fine hunting hawks, beautiful ponies with snowy coats in bright enamelled harness. The knight's presents were so many and frequent that they became the object of jokes around the Wooden Palace – there was not much to joke about just then – but it was evident that the knight either loved Meroot or needed her goodwill. It was clear, too, that he was a rich man.

I can still remember the set look on Gamal's face as the knight's servants arrived, day after day, bearing gifts.

'You know, they wish me to go with them – to live at Caerleon,' he said.

'You won't go?'

'I don't want to . . .' I knew of Gamal's loyalty to his mother, a loyalty I had only once ever seen waver.

The preparations at Castle Dore speeded up – the bards composed new songs and the smell of roasting meat pervaded everything. The kingdom was short of food yet the rules of hospitality demanded that guests should be richly entertained. On the night before the Grey Knight's arrival my father gave a feast for Meroot in the Great Hall and she sat beside him in the seat where my mother or I usually sat. Her pale face was flushed, her eyes sparkled, and there was an odd sort of triumph about her that troubled me. Sitting directly opposite to her I could not avoid her gaze, nor the need to make conversation.

'You will live at the house of the Grey Knight?' I asked her. She described it to me and it sounded very splendid. Yet gazing into her strange light eyes, so lacking in depth or feeling, I felt, as I had felt as a small child, that her apparent amiability concealed an intense hatred of me.

I remembered my father telling me of Meroot's longing, as a little girl, to outstrip him at everything – at running, at shooting with the bow, at climbing trees, or at the civilized arts of singing, or oration. For the first time I felt sympathy for Meroot – it was hard to be a girl in a royal family and see your younger brother preferred to you for no better reason than that he was a boy. I, who had no brothers, was far luckier than she – I am sure she thought this. Yet it was partly because I was a girl that Meroot could make her plot.

I slept fitfully, tossing and turning, and woke just before the cold, grey dawn. I got up quietly and went out, as I had done so often when restless or anxious, to walk around the ramparts and the big ditch beyond the ramparts. I hailed the sleepy sentries and began a slow pacing. It was bitterly cold, and I drew my cloak warmly around me, but I enjoyed watching the light gradually ascending over the valleys. But then, with a sense of shock, I saw the figure of a woman in a field outside, her face turned to the Wooden Palace, and I realized that it was Meroot. She could not see me – I was no more than a small face above the parapet and it was still fairly dark – and she went on with what she was doing, moving widdershins, holding up her hand and making signs in the direction of the palace, occasionally dipping her fingers into a bowl she held in her other hand. As the dawn gradually lightened I saw that her upraised hand was stained a dull red, that the bowl into which she dipped it must contain blood. I could not hear her voice, nor see her mouth move, but I had no doubt at all that she was uttering spells.

Chapter Nineteen

A Ritual

That day the Grey Knight arrived, celebrated by a trumpeter as he entered our gates, and surrounded by pages who carried more presents for Meroot, including a magnificent collar of pearls. He was received by my father and they spent half the day talking together. I met the knight when the evening brought us all together in the Great Hall.

He was a tall, handsome man, carrying, as many of the knights did, scars of battle on his face; in his case, they only added to his good looks. He had piercing black eyes, and when he was introduced to me, I felt as if he looked right through me and knew everything about me. For the first time since my return I felt afraid. The sight of Gamal's miserable face as he stood beside Meroot did not reassure me.

The wedding was celebrated with great splendour and as was our custom, the feast went on for days. Like most of the younger people, I got bored with the endless drinking and story-telling, and soon slipped away to talk and have fun. Freed from Meroot's supervision, Gamal and I spent a lot of time together. Quite often we were joined by Finbar who, despite myself, I was beginning to like. Gamal often played his flute, pausing from time to time to share the thoughts that troubled him.

'They'll make me go back to Caerleon with them,' he said. 'The trouble is I'm not old enough to refuse.'

'One of the knights could make you his squire,' Finbar suggested.

Gamal shook his head and both of us knew the reason why this was unlikely; if Meroot wanted him to accompany her none of the knights would wish to defy her.

'Do you think now that Meroot is married she will give up her plans for Castle Dore – you know, the ones you told me about that time at the shore?' (This was not quite honest of me. The memory of Meroot cursing us all in the winter dawn did not suggest that her ambitions had changed.)

Gamal shook his head and flushed.

'She has never forgiven your father – her younger brother – for inheriting the kingdom and taking it from her. She believes that it is rightly hers, and eventually mine.' He hesitated for a long while. 'She thinks only of how to get it back. She will not forgive me for refusing to help her. I think that is why she bore me, and why she insists I must be a soldier. So that somehow I can avenge her.'

'What will she do to get what she believes is hers? Will she fight for it, or will she prefer to use spells?' I tried to keep my voice as even as possible, as if we were discussing something that did not matter very much.

Gamal shrugged.

'I have no doubt she is using spells already. As to war . . . I do not know.'

'For a moment, the other night, I felt sorry

131

for Meroot,' I said. 'It is not fair that she was robbed of the throne – I should not like it if a younger brother was preferred before me – if I wanted to be queen, that is.'

'But she swore loyalty to King Mark, as we all did. He has been good to us and . . . you are my friend.'

I put out a hand and grasped Gamal's.

'In any case – curses are no way to get what you want.' So Gamal really did think, as I did, that Meroot's curse was what ailed the country.

It was a great relief when Meroot and the Grey Knight rode back to Caerleon along with their retinue of servants. The knight's servants had been rude and arrogant, and the feast had strained the slender resources of Castle Dore. Though, of course, I watched Gamal ride away with a sad heart. My friend and ally had left us.

Yet almost immediately I was distracted by a new piece of information. Visiting my mother I found her in a strange state, both elated and anxious.

'Ninnoc, it is unmistakable . . . I am to have another baby!'

I knew that she had longed to have another child, and that although she had loved me, her only daughter, she had felt somehow to blame for not providing the warrior-heir that kings preferred. I also knew that if she did have a boy, it meant that I would never become queen. I felt a pang of jealous rage. I tried to crush it down beneath the protective feelings I had about my mother.

'Don't tell anyone for as long as possible in case Meroot finds out,' I cautioned.

'That is why I am afraid,' said Erlain, her great

grey eyes filled with dread. 'That she may know already and have damaged my child.'

'You used the clearwater?'

'Yes. Every day.'

'It will be all right. This comes at a good time. It will comfort people that something – someone – can live and grow despite Meroot's curse.'

I was giving a lot of thought to Meroot's curse just then, and as a result I was sleeping badly. My nightmares were about Meroot, clad all in grey, and, more terrible, of a huge unwinking eye watching me through a hole in a wall. If only Euny were at home, I kept thinking, to give me advice. How could I undo the curse, and turn Meroot's corrupting, killing hate into the love that made all things grow?'

I turned over in my mind all that I had been taught. 'Earth, air, fire, water, those are your allies,' Euny had said.

I planned the ritual and asked my mother if she would accompany me. Next morning I woke with a sense of fear – I felt as if I was directly challenging Meroot – but I got up, put on Euny's crescent moon necklace, and my *doran's* cloak, and lifted Moon down on to my shoulder. Erlain and I went out together to the place beyond the walls where I had seen Meroot. I stood still and thought of the mother goddess before whom Euny had bowed in her shrine high on the tor.

Then I took earth and crumbled it between my fingers.

'Mother, let this earth yield crops to feed our animals and food for our children. Let the plants flower and the trees bear fruit. Let sun and rain make it rich and fertile, and let no human blood be spilt upon it.'

I took water and poured it out upon the ground.

'Mother,' I said, 'let our springs and streams and rivers run pure so that all may drink. Let this water wash away the curse of violence.'

I lit a small fire.

'Mother, let this fire burn away all that is wicked and corrupt.'

Finally, I stood looking up into the dark sky.

'Mother, let the air of this place not be filled with cries of pain.'

I turned to Erlain, the mother whom I knew and loved. Putting my hands gently on her belly, I thought of the little baby within.

'Mother, keep this one safe,' I said. 'May this child be born strong and healthy and grow up in a kingdom that knows peace.'

Then, as Angharad and Euny had taught me, I danced the dance that is the harmony of all creation, and as I did so I uttered the great words — ZALUSTAN — XOSINGREST — MARIGBOLUNIS — FEGMAL — LUSTOOMON — WEFWARNO — which keep sorrow and sickness within bounds. Finally I bowed low in the direction of the Wooden Palace.

When it was over, I felt desperately tired, almost too weary to climb the path into Castle Dore. I had given my strength to the anti-curse and it left me feeling weak and afraid. Yet it was with a sense of pleasure and relief that I noticed, as we returned, that the rooks were rising from the trees on one side with noisy cries, and flapping indignantly away.

Within a few weeks it was plain that something was very different in the kingdom. The animals began to eat, the ewes and cows and horses to conceive, and the people to regain their old vitality.

My mother had a new piece of information for me.

'Ninnoc, I don't know what you will say. The astrologers tell me that the baby will be a boy!' Again I felt that pang of jealousy and anger. It had not been difficult to utter a *doran's* blessing upon the new baby — I could not possibly wish my mother any harm — yet I knew that in my heart I had hoped the baby would be a girl.

The winter months slipped away and the sun returned. That year we had a wonderful spring. The air seemed full of the calling of birds and the woods shone with primroses, violets and bluebells. Trees and hedgerows were covered in blossom, the sowing produced strong green shoots, and the lambing was the best we had ever had. After the fear and darkness of the winter, people were lighthearted and joyous — they were thin and short of food after their ordeals, but their eyes were full of hope, and my father walked with a light step. Meroot had gone and her curse had gone with her.

Chapter Twenty

Flying

I heard nothing of Gamal for many weeks and I missed him sorely. It worried me that if Meroot's schemes were defeated then loyal Gamal might be made to suffer for it in some way – I could scarcely imagine that he was happy in the house of Meroot and the Grey Knight, knowing well that the best parts of his childhood had all been at moments when he was away from his mother.

Now that the immediate danger to Castle Dore had been averted, there seemed no real task for me there, nothing worthy of my energies or of my training as a *doran*. Euny, I reckoned, might be back by now from her visit to Angharad. I thought that I would go and see her, tell her of what had passed since I left her, and see whether she would give me any guidance about my future. Goodness knows, she was obstinate enough in what she would, and would not, talk about, yet it was my experience of her that when my need was urgent enough she would relent and tell me what I had to know.

I suppose I could have taken my pony and travelled faster, yet it seemed proper to approach Euny on foot as I had done in the past. With little more than a change of clothing I made my way to Euny's hut once again, navigating by the tor, passing through the forest without the fear I had once known. If she was not at home, I thought, I could spend a day or two at the hut and return, though I would be very disappointed not to see her. I was delighted, at the end of my long walk, to see the smoke rising from her hut. Just as if she were awaiting me after an afternoon of herb gathering, she was sitting in her rocking-chair, and one of her strange-smelling soups was bubbling on the fire.

I could tell from her smile that she was very glad to see me, though, as ever, she did her best to hide her pleasure.

'Nothing better to do, I suppose,' she said with a sniff.

'I was longing to see you, and I need your advice,' I said.

'I knew,' she said. 'I made the soup because you were coming.'

'How did you know?' I asked, more for the pleasure of hearing what she would say than because I doubted her.

'I dreamed it,' she said airily.

I had my familiar sense of being surprised by Euny – of always being on the wrong foot yet of rather enjoying it – and I laughed to myself as I sat down by the hearth. It seemed a long time since the day I had sat there with my swollen ankle and wept at the misery of becoming her apprentice.

Over supper I told her of the anti-curse and how well it had worked. She listened attentively, her dark eyes watching me, and when I had finished she gave a nod of approval.

'But I do not think Meroot has finished with us,' I added. 'I believe she means to take my father's kingdom by one means or another. There is the baby, too. If my mother has a boy, then I shall not become queen.' I tried to say this calmly, without feeling, but Euny was not deceived.

'You're jealous!' she said, with a cackle, pointing her finger at me.

For a moment I hated her, then I nodded.

'I am,' I said.

Euny was silent for a long time. I had forgotten how slowly life moved around her.

'It is time to fly,' she said at last. I knew that flying was an important adventure in the *doran* world – that it was a way of discovering where one's true vocation lay. I took a deep breath – the idea scared me – and said, 'When?'

'The day after tomorrow. You will need to fast.'

In order to fly you had to have a special ointment spread all over your skin. Then you sat very still and concentrated, usually with the help of your teacher, and if all went well you found yourself in another place. What you had to do there was to keep your eyes and ears open, and if you did it properly, then you often learned about the future, not so much ordinary details about what might happen to you – the sort that fortune-tellers go in for – as a sense of the shape and meaning of it. It was easy to get frightened and to will oneself back into ordinary life long before the end. I was determined that whatever I saw I would wait for the flying dream to leave me of its own accord rather than run away from it.

The day of fasting seemed very long but as night-time came Euny helped me bathe and then anointed me all over with the brown ointment, of which she kept a jar on a shelf. Then the two of us waited, standing face to face before the fire, our eyes fixed on one another. I felt a little sick, a little faint, but Euny willed me to stand upright while I waited for the moment of change. I would have given a lot to be somewhere else just then, but I tried to be calm and to wait. What changed everything was a sound like a tremendous cracking – the sort of sound a tree makes if it is snapped off in a winter gale – a noise so loud that I felt I lost consciousness for a moment. Then there was a strong pulling sensation as if a hurricane was blowing me away and I was whirling through space so fast that it was hard to breathe. Not for long.

Almost at once, it seemed, I was in a dark place which reminded me of my old dream. I could not seem to see at all but I was running – over sharp, slippery stones – and something was coming after me making a noise of splashing and snuffling. An appalling stench was in my nostrils, one which I felt I ought to remember, but could not quite identify. Almost before the horror of this overtook me, the vision changed. Now I could see, and what I saw was Gamal's face, quite clearly, but it was upside down. At the same time I heard the sound of a child crying.

Then once again the pulling feeling had me in its power. I was being lifted, dragged, blown off the earth and had to submit again to being whirled in space. From high up in the sky I looked down upon an island, and then, immediately as it seemed, I stood upon the island in front of a house. The house was white and stood upon a sort of inland cliff. I entered it and there was a great hearth in the centre of the room, the heart, I thought, of a place full of peace. Behind it were shelves full of liquid and when I looked out I could see a garden with neat rows of herbs. On the other side I could see that the land fell away, and in the distance was a view of village and sea and shore. Feeling almost as if I was trespassing in someone's house, and the owner might come home and catch me, I sat in a big chair by the hearth, watched thoughtfully by an owl – not Moon – who perched on a shelf. As I did so, my fears subsided. I knew that this was my chair and my house, that I fitted it perfectly and was completely comfortable – that this was the place in the world that I was seeking. It was a place in which there was no dread. From it I returned, after a while, to Euny's hut.

'I've found it,' I reported with joy to Euny.

'What?'

'The place where I must be.'

'Where is it?'

I described to her the house and the island, the inland cliff and the distant sea, and she nodded.

'I think I know where it is.'

'Where?' I was breathless.

'If the flying dream wanted you to know that it would have told you,' she said maddeningly. 'In any case that is far in the future. Was that all you saw?'

Much less happily I told her of the terror that had pursued me in the tunnel, of Gamal's face, and of the sound of crying. She looked grave.

I was puzzled by flying dreams and what they meant.

'Do they make something happen to you, or are they what would have happened anyway?' I asked Euny.

'There is a part of you,' said Euny, 'which knows

the future as well as it knows the past. It is not concerned with time. So that if you consult that part, which is what the flying ointment does, it can give you a memory of the future, just as your ordinary memory tells you about the past.' She hesitated, her eyes fixed on mine as both of us struggled with this memory, a very fleeting and vague memory in my case, of the future. I had a sense that something was being asked of me, some act of love or generosity that felt unbearably difficult.

'Something must be given up,' I heard myself say to Euny, and she nodded encouragingly, as if that was just what she had seen herself, and she quoted under her breath a *doran* poem about seeking with 'purity of spirit'.

'How do you mean?' I asked, but she simply stared at me in reply, as if she had said quite enough.

'Gamal? How does he come into it? Why is he upside down?'

'Your love and friendship for him will be tested. Meroot, or perhaps the Knight – they have power over Gamal at present.' Euny's eyes looked past me now, as if painfully fixed on the future.

'And the terror in the tunnel?' I finally asked reluctantly.

'You are a *doran*,' said Euny. 'A *good* one. I have seen to that. To be able to encounter evil, naked evil, that is your business. Not every day, not often, but when it is necessary. And now that you have found your place – through the flying – that makes it much easier. That is your centre – it waits for you, and one day it will find you.'

I returned to Castle Dore scarcely knowing

whether to feel pleased or sad. The joy and calm I had felt in my dream house with the great hearth taught me that one day I would truly find my place and my own peace in the world, which is the same as finding oneself. How could anyone not rejoice at that? Yet somewhere in my life – presumably before I found my way to the island – lay the prospect of terror, with the unknown significance of the crying child. I didn't like that thought at all.

So, not very cheerfully, I set off on the long walk home. It felt comforting to see dear Castle Dore looking particularly beautiful as the evening sun shone upon its steep walls and low roofs.

'Your father wants you,' Erith said, as I washed off the dust of my journey and changed my gown.

Something different about the king's face struck me as soon as I came into his apartment, and without asking anything about my journey he came straight to the point.

'I have heard from Meroot,' he said, not beating about the bush. 'Gamal is proposing marriage to you.'

142

Chapter Twenty-One

Finbar and I

I was so surprised that I sat down on a stool and stared dumbly at the king.

'We're not old enough,' I said at last. I knew very well, of course, that children of my age, particularly royal children, did get married, but because Gamal was my friend whom I had always known, it had never occurred to me to think of him as a possible husband.

'In many ways it would be a good solution,' the king went on, ignoring my remark. 'Meroot, though she does not complain, I am sure has minded that my birth robbed her of the throne. By this marriage of cousins she would feel gratified, and Castle Dore would have the protection of a warrior.'

'As well as of a *doran*,' I said crossly. At that moment I felt hurt and angry that my father would so clearly have preferred a boy as his successor. 'But if mother has a boy, Meroot won't get her wish anyway.'

'That is true. We must consider both possibilities.'

'Well, why don't we wait and see? There's no hurry, is there?'

I could see the king trying to decide how much to tell me, though the gravity of his expression told me much before he spoke.

'I am told,' he said, 'that the Grey Knight is pressing the countryside for soldiers. No-one is quite sure,' his tone was very dry, 'what he is training them for, but the rumour is that he means to attack Castle Dore.'

I knew how painful this news must be to him for several reasons, but I also saw how it affected my own position. The Grey Knight had let the news leak out that he might attack us, but at the same time a marriage was suggested between Gamal and me. If I agreed, or my father agreed on my behalf, there would be no war, but if not . . .

'Although you love Aunt Meroot, and you believe she loves you, you think she would let the Knight attack us?' I felt angry at his blindness about his sister. He did not reply, but a look of mingled shame and pain crossed his face.

'You *like* Gamal,' he said. 'He has been your dearest friend.'

I thought of my dear friend with his honest eyes and his truthful tongue.

'I take it there is no word from Gamal himself,' I said. There was not. Both of us fell silent, each thinking our thoughts. I was beginning to wonder why the flying dream had given me no hint of marriage, when the king startled me out of my reverie with his next words.

'Your Aunt Meroot suggested that you should visit Caerleon, and, not to offend her, I accepted the invitation on your behalf.'

I reacted to this news with shock and disbelief.

'Father, these people wish to fight us, maybe to seize Castle Dore and take over your throne, and you send me to visit them!'

'There will be no danger to the kingdom if you marry Gamal, and besides, Meroot will take care of you.' Nothing, I could see, would ever convince my father that Meroot was not to be trusted. All the same I thought I would try once more.

'I don't trust Meroot. She is a dangerous woman. All she wants is to put Gamal on the throne. I don't want to go to Caerleon.'

My father's face grew dark with rage but he would not argue with me.

'You will do as I say.'

I got up, inclined my head in the gesture that etiquette demanded, and went out. Without hesitation I went in search of my mother.

'You know about the marriage suggestion? And that Meroot has invited me to Caerleon?'

She nodded, ashamed.

'I am sure the king knows that it is wrong, but he fears to lose the kingdom to the Grey Knight's men.'

'So I am to be the sacrifice?' I asked bitterly.

'We women are not asked whom we will marry. I was lucky that I loved your father. You could do worse than Gamal.'

'And become the tool of Meroot and the Grey Knight?'

In my anger I went out and paced around the Great Ditch as so often before. What I resented most was having no control over my life, of being a mere pawn, indeed a lost pawn, in the game being played between Meroot and my father. Suddenly an arrow whistled past my ear. I looked up and there, fifty paces away, was Finbar grinning at me.

'That's dangerous,' I said crossly. In my heart I had never quite forgiven Finbar.

'Let me come with you.'

'What?'

'Let me come with you to Caerleon.'

'How on earth do you know about that?' Castle Dore was always alive with gossip, but I imagined my father had kept his moves fairly secret.

'I have been your father's messenger.'

'Why do you want to go?'

'Because I am Gamal's friend and because . . .' with a slightly nervous gesture he looked up at the walls around us. He knew, as I did, that someone lying just the other side of the mound could hear every word that was said, while remaining unseen. 'Is there somewhere we could talk in private?'

We returned to my apartment and sat there together as Gamal and I had done so often in the past.

'I carried a message for your father to Caerleon. It is a grim place. Naturally, when my business was done, I asked to see Gamal. Meroot said at first that I could not see him, but I said, (he grinned his cheerful smile), 'that I had a message for him from you that you had said I must deliver directly to him. She kept me waiting for ages and then Gamal came . . . he was brought . . . into the room where I was.' A look of fear crossed Finbar's brown face. 'He was . . . I don't know words for it . . . he was *not there*. He was like somebody sleep-walking. I am not even sure he knew me.'

'He was ghosted,' I said.

'What's that?'

'It is when you take the spirit out of somebody so that you can control them, body and soul.'

'Can it be cured?'

'Maybe.'

There was a long silence between us. Now, instead of resenting the fact that I was forced to visit Caerleon, I wanted to go, to reach Gamal and see what ailed him. How bravely he must have resisted, for them to resort to such a desperate measure.

'Could you cure him?'

'Perhaps. Going there . . . trying to help Gamal . . . might be dangerous, you know?'

Finbar nodded, as if the thought of danger gave him pleasure. I was surprised to hear myself add, 'It would be good to have you with me . . . someone who cares about Gamal as much as I do.' It was an effort to say this.

Finbar hesitated and then said, 'I am sorry I was rude to you that time at Euny's. I don't know why I did it. I was young and very silly. It was not the way to treat the king's daughter, and it was ungallant of me. I like you a lot, and I'd like to help you on this visit. You can trust me, and you will need people you can trust there.'

He was not alone in feeling this. That night when I mentioned the visit to Erith she said almost the same thing.

'You know I never liked your Auntie Meroot. I don't trust that one as far as I can see her.' I sketched for her Finbar's description of Gamal.

'That poor boy!' Erith said indignantly.

In the days that followed I made my preparations. I rehearsed various spells in my head, I made several flasks of clearwater, I took Euny's black egg from its wrappings, and I prepared herbs with a number of magic properties. I carried a little package of titbits for Moon – Erith was disbelieving when I said that I must take the owl, but I felt quite sure that I must – and of course, I took my cloak and my moon amulet, which nowadays I wore all the time.

The little band that set off for Caerleon included not only Finbar, but four soldiers, a bard (to sing the praises of the young couple), and an astrologer magician called Winan. (I had scant respect for the official magic of my father's court, but I felt that if I apparently consulted a charlatan and fraud like Winan it might lull Meroot into a sense of false security about my knowledge.)

So, not without fear, I finally set off for Caerleon.

The journey took us several days but the weather was fine. We lay down at night in a meadow or a wood – wrapping ourselves in our blankets we slept under the stars and woke in the cold dawns to the scent of the soldiers' fire and the smell of bacon cooking. Between Finbar and myself a special closeness sprang up – we were drawn together by our love of Gamal, by our sense of the dark magic that threatened all of us and the dangers that might lie ahead. Our love and trust in one another, together with my largely untried magic, were nearly all the protection that we had. I insisted that he should use the clearwater. Finbar laughed, but I suspected that he was glad enough of whatever protection it might afford.

Now that I had time to think about it I was surprised at how my feelings towards Finbar had changed. The rude boy who had hurt my feelings and made me jealous was now quite different – a companion whose loyalty had been proved, whose laughter and jokes were very comforting, whose brilliant blue eyes seemed to me to see farther than most.

Even Finbar was silent, however, at the moment when we first saw the outline of the castle of Caerleon against the sky. I suspect he was wondering, as I was, whether any of us would come out of it alive, or at least without damage of spells.

I put on my cloak, which made me feel safer. As we got nearer to Caerleon we saw how grim and fortified it was, and I speculated what Gamal had felt the first time he approached it with the Grey Knight and Meroot. The guards on the gate did not challenge us, and we rode through and into a courtyard where our horses were taken from us.

Chapter Twenty-Two

Trapped

In my father's house it would have been the practice for the guests to have been shown immediately into his presence, or, if that were impossible, to be greeted by an ealdor and offered refreshment. In the Grey Knight's house, in contrast, we were left standing in the courtyard, tired and dirty as we were after our journey. At Castle Dore you were always aware of life going on about you – you could hear chatter, laughter, singing, as people went about their work. At Caerleon there was an ominous silence that grew as we waited, a silence so oppressive that our conversation fell to a whisper.

'Do you feel we are being watched?' Finbar asked me, almost whispering in the deadly silence. I nodded. The same thought had occurred to me. Somewhere, I knew, from the stairways and balconies above us, eyes were looking down coldly upon us. I shivered, and was glad of my warm covering.

At that moment, however, a servant appeared, and bore away all my possessions to the apartment I would occupy, and the soldiers to the barracks. He tried to shepherd Finbar out with the soldiers, but Finbar stood fast, and I said firmly, 'Finbar comes with me.'

'My lady asked only for you,' the servant said nervously.

'And I will not go without Finbar. I will explain it to your lady.'

Meroot was sitting in a huge chair on a dais in the middle of a long room, which gave her the appearance of a queen awaiting her subjects. Herbs were strewn on the floor and gave the room a scented, spicy smell. The great black hound sat at her feet watching us alertly. Meroot's thin body was dressed in a silk gown of brilliant red, decorated at the neck with a chain of flashing stones. She waited until I had advanced several steps into the room and I was very conscious that she was studying me minutely. I had the strongest feeling that she knew that I had the protection of my *doran's* cloak, and probably that my skin had been bathed with clearwater. Then, as if she had only just noticed me, she rose to her feet with a small cry of simulated delight. She held out her arms to me, kissed me, though not warmly, and drew me to a seat beside her grand chair. It was placed, I noticed, on a lower step.

'You remember Gamal's friend, Finbar,' I said, indicating him, and Meroot gave him a bleak stare.

'I had hoped that we might speak alone,' she said.

'There is nothing that Finbar may not hear,' I said. 'He is my father's messenger.'

She hesitated, and then, plainly not wishing to cross me so early in our meeting, said, 'Very well.'

'We were kept waiting by your servants,' I said, 'and we need to wash after our journey.'

'Later, later,' she said indifferently.

There was a pause, and again I had the unpleasant sensation of being watched. I looked around the room. There were hanging tapestries which might have concealed a watcher, and I noticed that a door at the far end of the room was ajar.

'Where is Gamal?' I asked in a loud voice. By all means let any eavesdropper hear the conversation.

'He is unwell,' she said.

I stared into the sandy lashes with an expression that showed plainly enough that I knew this statement to be a lie.

'So what ails him?' I asked.

'He has a rash and a fever,' she replied. 'In case of infection we are keeping him alone.'

'I could help perhaps. I am trained in healing skills.'

A look of great contempt crossed Meroot's face.

'I have no doubt that you know all that the old wives have to teach.'

I controlled my temper, remembering the need to find a way to help Gamal.

'You know that Gamal's choice of you, Ninnoc, as his wife, has brought great joy to the Grey Knight and myself. As my brother's daughter you were always dear to me, and now we shall move into a closer friendship to which I look forward with happiness.'

'And Gamal? What does he feel?'

'How can you ask? You know that he has always adored you.'

'We have been friends . . .'

Her eyes flickered hypnotically. She had an oddly snake-like quality, I thought.

'You will wish to see your room. It is what we

152

call the eastern apartment. Finbar will have a room in the barracks.'

'Finbar,' I said, 'is part of my retinue and must have a room near to me. My father was concerned about my taking so long a journey virtually alone, and I promised him that Finbar would be my bodyguard and stay always within earshot.'

Meroot's eyes flickered again.

'You think yourself in danger in the Grey Knight's house?'

'There are dangers everywhere.'

'When I was a girl,' Meroot said icily, 'it would have caused gossip about a girl to have a young man sleeping within earshot.'

'My honour, and Finbar's,' I said, 'are beyond doubt. And I am still a child. I am surprised at you, Aunt Meroot.'

Finbar had listened to this exchange with his habitual look of faint amusement, but he flashed an admiring look at me when it became clear that I had won the argument. I was very relieved to know that in that sinister castle he would be close at hand.

The two of us went with Meroot to the eastern apartment. It was large and pleasant with a big, silk-hung bed. There were fine tapestries of gods and goddesses; in the one opposite to the bed a goddess who seemed to be the spirit of spring was strewing flowers over a bare winter landscape. A servant had unpacked my baggage and everything was stored neatly away. I lifted Moon out of the bag I was carrying and set him, sleepy as ever, on a beam.

I noticed that another room opened off the chamber and asked for the door to be opened. I sensed the servant's reluctance to unbolt the door, during which I thought I could detect the sound of movement in the room next door. Finally, Meroot nodded, and a manservant opened the door, on to a small, bare apartment, in which there would be plenty of room to place a bed for Finbar. I noticed a clean patch in the heavy dust on the floor, as if a chair had stood there, very close to the door of my chamber, and had now been taken away. My guess was that someone had been preparing to spy.

Finally Meroot went away with her servants, leaving Finbar and me alone. We looked searchingly at each other but knew better than to speak our thoughts.

'I need to wash and to rest,' I said, 'and so will you. But I would like to see the environs of Caerleon before dark. Later we will ride together.'

Finbar nodded and went out.

When we did meet there was something I needed to report to him immediately.

'They took the clearwater,' I told him. 'I questioned the servant and she swore that the flasks had not been in the baggage.'

'That leaves us unprotected,' Finbar said, with a grave face. I noticed that he no longer thought the clearwater a silly fad of mine.

'Not at all,' I said cheerfully. 'Look!' And I produced a flask from under my cloak.

'I brought us one each, just to be sure. Use it carefully.'

Finbar plainly felt comforted by the clearwater and I, for my part, was comforted by Finbar's gaiety and confidence. Even in this dreadful place he could make jokes.

With the rest of the retinue we attended the formal dinner that Meroot gave in welcome. I had taken a lot of trouble with my appearance, and was slightly dismayed when, just before I went to the hall, Moon clambered up my arm and sat firmly on my shoulder. I lifted him gently off, saying, 'No, Moon,' but he returned imperturbably and I knew that he meant to accompany me. I felt that I must look very odd when I entered the hall, but when I sat down Moon hopped on to the floor and dozed off again under my chair. I sat beside the Grey Knight. He was beautifully dressed in velvet and fur and scented with a sweet rich oil. (Did the scent conceal some other, less pleasant, odour? I suspected that it did.) As I soon discovered from his conversation, the Knight was a well-educated man. He spoke to me of fine manuscripts he had seen, of his reading in the Latin authors, of the astronomical wisdom of the ancients; he was a very courteous gentleman, and I must say I was charmed by him. He had huge, dark eyes that I found very attractive, only every time I looked into them they reminded me of someone. It bothered me that I could not think who it was. I retired for the night more than a little under the Knight's spell.

Next morning we were taken to see the Grey Knight's soldiers practising on a nearby field. I was appalled by their numbers – they were a small army – and I knew that I was intended to be impressed by this display of might.

Three days passed. Meroot said that it was such a pity that Gamal was too ill to meet me on this visit but that she could not risk my catching his fever. There was nothing, however, to prevent us making all the necessary plans for the wedding, though it was sad that Gamal and I might not meet again until the actual day of the ceremony.

I did not know where Gamal's apartment was, closely as I watched the servants for clues, but I did know that Meroot and the Knight had their private rooms in the western wing of the castle.

So it was that I formed the desperate plan of visiting the rooms in Meroot's absence, to see whether I could find Gamal, or simply discover some secret about Meroot – I knew not what – that would help us to save him. Every afternoon, I observed, she and the Knight rode out together, yet I knew that her servants might be at work in her absence.

After the mid-day meal I had pleaded a headache and a need to rest, and had gone to my room. Later, knowing that Meroot would have left, I put on my *doran's* cloak, and with my heart beating quite fast I went to the western apartments. Meroot had a suite of rooms, and in the first of them her fat servant was asleep upon a day-bed, snoring loudly. I slid silently past her and into another room with an open door. This was a day-room, comfortably appointed, and on the far side of it was Meroot's sleeping-chamber. There was nothing of interest there except a troubling smell. Partly it was the smell of Meroot's dog – I was surprised that she allowed such a large dog in her room and also that its smell lingered even in its absence, though I was relieved that she had not left it behind to guard her apartment. Yet beyond the dog smell there was another smell that I half-recognized, but could not place. There was no time to think about it, however. When I opened a door on the far side of the chamber I found myself in a work-room full of flasks and jars. A cock was in a crate on the floor and began to protest at the sight of me. I recognized many herbs whose uses I knew well, but everything was placed tidily on its shelf and there was nothing to indicate which of the jars were in use. Meroot's leather stick stood against the wall, and I picked it up and examined it with interest. It had the look and feel of a magical object, but I could not imagine what Meroot used it for.

Yet another door opened out of this room, and without much hope of finding further clues about Meroot I opened it. For a wild moment I simply could not take in what I saw, it was so extraordinary. For there, sitting up in bed and staring straight at me, wild-eyed, was Gamal! Not only did his face show no sign of recognition of me, Ninnoc, but he seemed unaware that anyone had come into the room. I crossed to the bed and took his hand.

'Gamal! It is I, Ninnoc. Do you remember?'

But as if he was deaf, blind, and without feeling, Gamal continued to stare straight ahead of him. I squeezed his hand, touched his face, talked some more to him, but I might as well have talked to a chair. Yet I could feel that his hand trembled, that he was sweating, that his body gave off a foreboding smell of fear. I longed to stay with him, and spend longer trying to talk to him, but I knew that I could not risk it. Quietly I slid out of his room and began the journey back through Meroot's rooms towards the corridor and safety. I had got as far as Meroot's sleeping-chamber when to my horror, I heard Meroot's voice loudly scolding her servant. I could not escape!

I was so frightened when I heard Meroot's voice coming nearer that at first I could not move. Then, very quickly, I began to retreat backwards towards Gamal's room and there, without thinking about it, I crawled under the bed. I was well hidden by the hanging draperies of the bed, but I was shaking with terror at the thought of being caught by Meroot. I had no idea why she had returned early from her ride but I feared that somehow she had guessed what I had done.

She came into the room so quietly that at first I was not even sure she was there. I scarcely dared to breathe as I waited for her to lift the draperies and expose me. Then I heard her walk across the room and pour some water into a goblet. She walked back to the bed and it sounded as if she was giving the water to Gamal to drink. There was a clink as she put the goblet down, then a long silence. After an interminable wait Meroot, to my horror, said, 'You can come out from under the bed, Ninnoc.'

Red-faced, I crawled out, saying the first thing that came into my head.

'I thought perhaps I could help Gamal. Being a healer.'

Meroot looked at me with a mixture of amused contempt and anger, that made me feel not at all like a *doran* but like a very silly little girl.

'If we need your help, Ninnoc, we shall ask for it. In the meantime I shall speak to your father about your appalling manners, and suggest that he teaches you the rudiments of what it means to be a guest. Since you have forfeited that right I shall treat you as what you are – a naughty child. Go to your room. We shall not expect to see you at table until tomorrow.'

I went to my apartment, fuming at Meroot's speech. Yet despite my anger I knew that there was something much more important at stake than my hurt feelings. I could not forget Gamal's staring eyes and blank white face.

Chapter Twenty-Three

The Plan

When I did not appear for our evening ride Finbar came in search of me, and it was a relief to be able to tell him what had happened. Before I spoke a word he went round the tapestries poking them and looking behind them, and even then we spoke to each other in whispers. I could see that Finbar was impressed at my courage. I was pleased, too, that he decided that if I was to go without my dinner he would share my exile.

'I bet she only got so angry to distract you from what you had seen,' he said. 'She must be frightened now.'

'The trouble is that now she knows I know. What I long to do is kidnap Gamal and take him – I thought to Angharad's, it is less than a day's ride from here – where he could get better. But her guards would never let him through the gate.'

'Suppose we pretend that we have not noticed anything – that we believe her story about the fever. You agree to marry Gamal on the day she appoints. We leave and go home. Then we return secretly and steal Gamal away. They won't know we are coming back and he won't be guarded.'

'We would never get through the gate.'

'We might climb up the outside somehow,' he said doubtfully.

'And get Gamal out that way? In his present state?'

'What we really need is a path that leads into the heart of the house. They say that all such castles have a secret way in and out, so that if there is a siege the ealdors and their ladies can escape.'

We were both silent, trying to think how, even if such a path existed, it could possibly be discovered by us. The next day I begged Meroot's pardon, and after that I went out of my way to be nice to her, pretending to enjoy my stay and to take an interest in hawking, a hateful, bloody sport to which both she and the Knight seemed addicted. I could not decide whether or not she was taken in – I would catch her eyes resting thoughtfully upon me, but in the days that followed Finbar and I became extraordinarily good actors. We swallowed Meroot's thinly veiled insults, and the Grey Knight's cold speeches, with smiles and soft words. I proclaimed how excited I was at the prospect of marrying Gamal, and a date was set three months hence. I let Meroot believe that though at first I had thought I was too young, my father had prevailed on me to agree, and his word was law. Perhaps I overdid it; I don't know.

Meanwhile, Finbar and I spent more and more time in the countryside, searching in copses and on rocky outcrops for anything that looked like a cave that might lead into a passage. Armed with candles, tinderbox, and a makeshift lantern, we searched with ever-declining hope. On one such day – a rather hot day – we were sitting in a wood to give ourselves and our sweating horses a little shade, when I idly picked up a stick and twirled it in my fingers as we talked. Suddenly, to my great surprise, a familiar feeling ran through my hands and arms, and I felt the twig, of its own accord, move upwards. I gave an involuntary gasp and Finbar opened his eyes and saw the twig move. 'It's nothing,' I said, slightly embarrassed. 'It may mean that water runs beneath here, or that some precious stone . . .'

I broke off because Finbar sat up sharply, his brilliant eyes staring at mine.

'Water!' he said.

'What about it?'

'Water runs beneath the castle, does it not? There is a place in the foundations where the servants draw water from an underground stream. On my first visit, when I slept with the servants, I went there to wash myself, as we all did. An underground stream runs into the castle but it does not appear to run out again. So that it must stay underground for some distance, but then perhaps it emerges. If it does, that might be the way in, don't you think?'

We were both so excited by this idea that we set off at once, riding slowly along so that we could watch the action of the twig as we did so. It took us across several fields, and across a moor, and through a wood. I was just beginning to feel that this was foolish – that we might follow the indications of the twig for miles – when we began to hear the noise of a stream. There, tumbling out from beneath a rocky outcrop in a waterfall, was the water we had so faithfully followed.

Seen from below it was hard to imagine that there was any way in to the ground but we knew that we must at least explore the possibility. Tying up our horses in the wood, we slipped off our outer garments – we couldn't

afford to go back to Caerleon wet and bedraggled – and jumped, gasping, into the stream.
Once we were over the first shock, the water
was deliciously cool. We climbed some slippery,
weed-covered rocks at the side of the waterfall,
inching perilously up to the place where the
water emerged. For a distance about the length
of a man beside the waterfall was an expanse
of smooth rock – at some time, probably hun-
dreds of years before – the waterfall had been
wider and had worn away the rock. Then, as
we drew level with the top of the waterfall,
we saw what could not be seen from below –
that there was a hole, or cave, which it was
perfectly easy to enter. Both of us shouted with
triumph at the same moment.

Only when you entered it could you see that the
path wound backwards into the darkness, into
a rocky tunnel. On one side of it was a stony,
precarious path, and beside that ran the stream.
We smiled at each other and Finbar lit the candle
we had thoughtfully brought and put it into his
lantern. Picking our way with care we began to
walk along the underground tunnel, sometimes
passing through high rocky caverns, sometimes
having to bend low to avoid bumping our heads
on the roof. I felt excited, exhilarated, by our
discovery. If only it led to the castle!

Quite soon, I noticed something that surprised
me. It was that the moon amulet Euny had given
me gave out a subdued light of a delicate greenish
colour. Even without a lantern it gave enough
light, I thought.

Just as I was beginning to feel that the path
might end anywhere, and that, however interesting the tunnel, we were unlikely to be helping

163

Gamal, Finbar suddenly stopped and pointed excitedly at the upper part of the rock walls.

'What? What?' I said, unable to see anything unusual.

'It's red,' he said. 'The rock is red. Just like the rocks around the castle.'

The path led on for another five hundred paces or so and then it seemed to peter out, with the stream emerging apparently from a solid wall of rock.

'We shall have to dive,' said Finbar. 'I *think* that is the wall of the castle, and on the other side of it is the place where they draw water, but we need to find out.'

'Suppose we don't come up for a long time . . . suppose we cannot draw a breath . . .' my voice petered out.

I didn't at all fancy jumping into that cold, black stream and diving under the wall.

'There's bound to be *some* space above the water,' said Finbar, sounding pretty doubtful himself. Then he added, 'Do you want me to go and find out? Someone must do it, and there doesn't seem any alternative to trying this.' Just then, Gamal's white face, staring eyes, and shaking hand, came vividly into my mind.

'Let's stay together,' I said, more bravely than I felt. We dived. First Finbar went. Then, taking a huge breath, I dived after him, groping down the wall of stone which, to my huge relief, only went down a short distance beneath the water. Putting my arms above my head, I used the bottom of the wall to hold myself down – so that it became a sort of ceiling – and found that my feet had touched smooth rock and that I could walk along using my hands to prevent my head from bumping on the rock above me. Just as I was beginning to feel frightened that I would use up all my breath, the rock came to an end, I floated up to the surface and, shaking the water from my eyes, I could see light at the end of the tunnel, only about the distance of an arrow-shot away. Once again Finbar and I exchanged pleased, relieved smiles. As we bobbed along the stream the tunnel curved and opened out, and suddenly we could see two of the castle servants standing in the washplace scrubbing the linen. It was fortunate that they were too busy scrubbing and chattering to notice our arrival. Both of us turned with one accord and swam silently back the way we had come. We had found the way to save Gamal.

Now we were ready to make the plans for our departure. Remembering Euny's instructions to me I sewed myself a belt with small pouches in it to take the protections she had given me, and I wore the moon amulet round my neck. I chatted to Meroot about the wedding, and plans for the future, and still I wondered whether she believed me. The day came for kidnapping Gamal – a perfect summer day, to which I woke with a feeling of sickening fear inside me. I longed for it to be time to go, but I knew that I must appear calm and controlled, as if nothing unusual was in prospect.

I said farewell to Meroot with an affection I had never shown her in my life and exchanged courteous pleasantries with the Grey Knight. Our little party set off on the route home – in a different direction from that of the stream.

Somehow I had to persuade our retinue to leave us. Perhaps because all of us were so relieved to be away from Caerleon it did not seem difficult. I told them that I wished to visit my old teacher

Angharad and that I would join them in two days' time on the road. Scarcely believing our good luck Finbar and I cantered away, soon finding the track back to the wood and the waterfall.

The worst bit of that day was waiting for darkness to fall while both of us tried to talk of other things.

'I am glad to be having this adventure with you,' Finbar said. 'I trust you.' By now I trusted him too, though I was also very frightened at the thought of entering the castle at its very heart. Would there be guards outside Meroot's rooms? Would any of her servants wake up? Most terrifying of all, would Meroot or the Knight awaken as we passed through their bedchamber? Then, would Gamal come with us, and how difficult would it be to get him to walk? Suddenly something else occurred to me and I gasped.

'The dog, Finbar!' I said. 'What about the dog?'

'I'd already thought of that. There is a kennel outside in the stables and all the dogs are kept in there at night. I slept near it on my last visit and was always being woken up by their barking.'

'We cannot put clearwater on us before we go in case the water washes it off,' I said, raising another worry. 'I shall carry a flask of it for us to use as we get out of the water.'

Finbar nodded, not at all sorry, I thought, to have a little magic working for him. I suspected that, secretly, he was just as frightened as I was, though sometimes, when we discussed the adventure, his eyes would flash with a touch of the old, carefree Finbar.

Chapter Twenty-Four

The Escape

I suppose when we worry about things it is a way of planning for all the possible disasters in advance. What often seems to happen then is that those particular disasters never occur, but that others undreamed of do. It was like that in our rescue of Gamal.

Leaving our horses in the wood, as before, we set off along the tunnel again, though it felt very different setting off on a dark night instead of on a summer afternoon. I wore my *doran's* cloak and Euny's amulet. I would have given a lot to have been safely tucked up in bed instead – only the thought of Gamal's white face drove me on. An odd thing happened soon after we had entered the tunnel. There was a swish of wings about our heads and we both ducked, thinking for a second that it was a bat. But, to my astonishment, there was the great white sweep of Moon's wings in the air above us. (I had left Moon in his bag, hanging from my saddle, but opened the top thinking that he would wish to fly and forage.) Now he settled on my shoulder for the rest of the journey, clutching me hard when I slipped or stumbled, and sitting on my arm when the roof got low. It was oddly comforting, having his company.

We safely negotiated the dive, leaving Moon

behind in the cave. I solemnly instructed him to wait and he seemed to understand. Once inside the castle we heaved our dripping bodies up on to the bank, shook off the drops, anointed ourselves with clearwater and then set off, young and alone in the heart of that grim place, me clad in my shift and belt, Finbar wearing only a pair of trews. The amulet was our light. I could feel, or hear, my heart thumping through me, but I felt excited and cheerful, not terrified as I had expected.

There was no sign of a guard as we made our way to the western side. Softly we opened the door of the ante-chamber, which was empty. To my relief no servants lay snoring in the outer room and no hound was in sight. On, through Meroot's sinister workroom and then, much more terrifying, into Meroot's bedchamber. The two of us stood in the doorway for an instant, ready to run at any moment. (I found myself thinking how, if necessary, we could dash down the stairs, into the water and back into the tunnel before they could catch us.) But the only sound in the room was of quiet breathing. Moonlight shone in one corner of the room, though the rest was in darkness. Its rays illuminated something – the turquoise collar that the hound had worn, lying on a table as if only just taken off. As I saw the collar there, a hideous smell reached my nostrils and a piercing realization came to me – of who it was that I was reminded of, when the Knight looked into my eyes. It was a terrible shock, but I came back to my present errand when Finbar took my hand, and the two of us walked lightly forward into Gamal's room. We closed the door behind us and turned to look at Gamal, who was sitting up in bed staring in front of him exactly as he had done on my last visit. It was terribly uncanny. Did he never sleep?

Finbar threw back the covers of the bed, and eased Gamal out of it. He walked him across the room, and to our relief he seemed perfectly able to walk. Finbar looked at me, and I nodded – we felt so tuned to one another that night that there was no need of words between us – and one on each side of Gamal, we walked smoothly through Meroot's room, and through the other rooms, as silently as we had come. By the time we got to the steps my legs had begun to shake so badly that it was quite hard to keep going, but Gamal needed more help from us there and I collected myself.

Finbar and I had discussed at length how we would get Gamal into the tunnel. There was nothing for it but to push him under the water and, with one of us in front of him and one behind, swim him along as best we could. Our great fear was that, not understanding what was going on, he would struggle with us – a nasty prospect in that narrow space – but all went well. In fact I had a feeling that although Gamal's mind was not with us his body was responding as well as it could. We got him through, pushing and pulling him between us on to the bank in the tunnel. We hastily dressed, I pulled my cloak on and we set off once more along the path. To begin with I felt much safer, but gradually a hateful feeling of unease spread over me. Soon I traced it to its source – seeing the turquoise collar in the bedroom and realizing where I had seen the look in the Knight's eyes. Yet this did not endanger us at the moment.

Just then, however, the small, ancient voice of Moon began to speak in my ear.

'Run, run . . . Run fast!'

'Why, Moon, why?'

'He's coming, he's coming . . . Run, run . . .'

'Who's coming, Moon?'

'The dog . . . the dog . . . the dog . . .'

I turned desperately to Finbar who did not understand Moon's language and only heard owl noises.

'Moon says the dog is coming. We must run, Finbar!'

Finbar must have been tempted to argue with me, but he did not do so. Together we tried to run, each of us holding one of Gamal's arms, but, not participating at all, he slowed us to little more than a fast walk.

'We *must* run, Gamal,' I said to him desperately, but I knew my words meant nothing to him. We stumbled over the rough surface, slippery and sharp, and more than once one of us fell, yet despite the pain, and the dead weight of Gamal, we dared not go slower. I was still hoping, as I am sure Finbar was, that it was all a mistake when, suddenly, far behind us, I heard a terrifying bark, and, a few moments later, the sound of the dog panting and running and snuffling as it leaped over the rocks. It was only, however, as a choking, evil smell reached my nose, that it came back to me – the experience of terror in the tunnel that I had known in my flying dream. With mounting horror I heard the great hound draw closer, splashing through puddles, giving tongue to a monstrous baying sound which echoed like thunder in the rocky chamber.

Even as I heard the great dog draw closer I remembered with dismay that, in our haste, we had forgotten to re-anoint ourselves with clearwater

when we emerged from the water. What I knew
now – had known ever since I saw the collar in
the bedroom – was that the dog was the Grey
Knight in his magical form. It was the eyes of
the dog that I had remembered the evening I had
talked with the Knight and it was that which
gave me the baffling sense of recognizing him.
In the few seconds that it took me to think this,
I remembered in detail the conversation with
Trewyn – about how she had been threatened on
the road by a huge black dog who was an enemy
of Angharad in disguise. It was terrifying enough
to be chased by a huge and savage beast; it was
much worse when you knew that it had human
and magical powers as well.

The three of us continued helplessly at our
slow, stumbling run – though it was clear, at
least to me, that there was no hope of us outrun-
ning the dog. As the hound drew near, Finbar, in
a last desperate attempt to save us, indicated a
ledge above the path. Finbar leaped and scrambled on it, and standing below I tried desperately
to push Gamal up to him, while Finbar grabbed
Gamal's shirt and pulled on it. The shirt tore,
and Gamal dropped down on to me, knocking
the breath out of me so that for a moment I was
helpless.

Then, hearing Moon's little voice chant a litany
of 'Try again . . . try again,' I seized Gamal, and
with a strength which at other times would have
been impossible for me, I picked him up and lifted
and pushed him upwards towards Finbar. This
time Finbar caught Gamal beneath the arms and
somehow dragged him up to sit on the ledge beside him. The dog was now very near – the noise
was deafening. I did not know how to find the

strength to scramble up to the ledge – I was trembling so much. Whether Finbar managed to pull me – I remember his arms reaching down to me as my feet slipped and slithered on the sandy surface – or whether some help reached me from my *doran* allies, I do not know. But one moment I was staring hopelessly upwards and the next I stood on the ledge beside Finbar. To my surprise I was suddenly much less afraid. While Finbar pulled Gamal further back on to the ledge so that his legs no longer hung down, I pulled my cloak around me and turned to confront the terror that pursued us. I noticed that my amulet now burned with a clear red light.

In the brief time before the dog reached us, when I could see its great red tongue hanging out, its eyes rolling, hear its baying cries, I reached into my pouch and took Euny's black egg in my hand. Within moments the suffocating smell of the beast seemed to surround us, so that I felt I must choke. I was aware of it crouching to spring, of its huge paw reaching up to drag me from the ledge, of its claws penetrating my cloak and piercing my leg. At that moment I threw the egg.

Finbar and I later had different recollections of what happened next. I thought there was a sort of flash, but Finbar said that the air 'split', as he put it, in some indescribable way; what both of us watched, unbelieving, was a beast slowly changing into a man, as the black hound became the Grey Knight. The Knight was deathly pale, and he tottered on his feet, clutching his throat as if unable to breathe. Ignoring us, he struggled like that for some moments, his face turning blue with the effort, until he collapsed on the ground, rolling to and fro in a sort of agony. Grotesquely, the front of his grey tunic was covered in egg yolk, as if I had thrown a perfectly ordinary egg at him.

I was so fascinated by the spectacle that I could do nothing but stand and watch. Finbar, however, nudged me, 'Let's get away.' While the Knight gasped and struggled and groaned, we lowered, or dropped, Gamal over the edge, as if he had been a sack of corn, and then, still not taking our eyes off the Knight, we two scrambled down. Once more the three of us set off half-running, but this time there was no sound of pursuit, only the sound of Moon's wings as he glided along beside us.

Chapter Twenty-Five

Fever

It was not till late afternoon that we reached the valley by Angharad's house, deep in the Outland. All day, since we had only two horses, Finbar and I had taken it in turns to walk, and my right leg had gradually become very painful. The deep scratch, which the dog's claw had inflicted, was a livid purple, and the leg itself was beginning to swell. I have rarely felt so tired or so frightened in my life; it was as if all the terrors of the night had overwhelmed me, and all day I could not believe that we were not pursued. I could not stop turning round and looking over my shoulder, as if at any moment the dog would be chasing us once more. Finbar too, was pale and nervous, and spoke little.

All this was bad enough, but at one moment when my hand went to my neck to feel the comfort of Euny's amulet, I found nothing there. I groped frantically beneath my cloak, felt my neck where the leather thong had been, but it had gone, and the silver moon had gone with it. I stopped, appalled.

'It's gone. What shall I do? What *shall* I do?'

Finbar was kind and sympathetic, but I knew that he had no idea of the power of such a gift.

'We can't go back . . . There's nothing we can

do, Ninnoc.' I began to long passionately for Angharad's kindness and wisdom, for the comfort of her house and the pleasure of seeing her gentle face.

It was with near-despair, therefore, as we breasted the hill and moved down into the valley, that I noticed that no smoke came from her smoke-hole, that no wool hung drying on her walls. As we arrived at the house I knew in my bones that it was empty – that Angharad was away on a journey. I was so disappointed that I began to cry, sniffing back the tears so as not to make Finbar feel miserable too. I felt I could not go on.

Of course, it felt good to reach the house and to look once more upon the big room where I had learned to spin and to weave, and where Trewyn and I had worked and laughed. What was odd was that everything seemed ready for us – peats and wood piled beside the fire, fresh milk and bread as well as other food on the table, the loom itself with a shuttle full of green wool, as if at any moment Angharad might come in and take it up. That encouraged me – Angharad must mean to return soon, might be back that very night – and with a lighter spirit than I had felt all day I made one further exhausted effort, laid and lit the fire, and set about preparing a supper of porridge.

Finbar and I had not eaten for a day and once we had dined (and painstakingly fed spoonfuls of porridge into Gamal), we both cheered up at once. I had taken the precaution of fastening the bolts on Angharad's doors; sitting comfortably by the fire with Gamal safe between us, everything suddenly felt much better. Finbar and I smiled at one another.

'We did it!' he said softly to me.

I climbed into my old bed, and spread my *doran's* cloak on top of me. Fingering the long tear the dog had made in it I noticed something odd. The place in the front of the cloak where the tear began was the place where, all those months ago, I could not be bothered to go back to correct the mistake in the weaving.

'No-one will notice,' I had thought, and no-one had noticed. Yet it had given the dog his chance to wound me. My throbbing leg made me bitterly regret my carelessness.

I slept late the next morning – Gamal, Finbar said, never slept at all, but sat staring unseeingly in front of him. My leg had swollen badly in the night so that I could barely walk, and Finbar waited upon me and Gamal. Seeing my nervous concern to keep the door bolted all the time, Finbar was reassuring.

'Meroot could not possibly know that we are here you know. Nor the Knight. If he survived, which seems unlikely.'

I wished I believed him. I had been trying to remember overheard conversations between Euny and Angharad about the ability of *dorans* and sorcerers to 'smell out' their enemies. My own heightened sense of smell since the *doran* ceremony made it seem only too likely that a person more experienced with magic than I, might develop advanced skills of this kind. I could not recall exactly what my teachers had said, but my impression was that, though it might take a while, a quarry was always found in the end. My fervent hope was that Angharad would return before Meroot found us.

In the meantime we must care for Gamal. It

was unnerving having him sit with us all the time, speechless and unseeing. I loved the tender way Finbar washed his face and hands, combed his hair, tidied his clothes, and fed him. Lying, more or less helpless, beside the hearth, bothered by increasing pain in my leg and full of fears and dark thoughts, I decided to distract myself by thinking about Gamal's problem and how he might be healed. I traced my way back through the long rigmaroles about healing that Euny had drilled into me in our last weeks together.

'What we have to do,' I told Finbar, 'is find "a path to his heart" — that's what the *dorans* say. We must think of something that matters so much to him that it will lure him out of his hiding place.'

'Hiding place?' said Finbar looking thoughtfully across at Gamal. 'You mean that he is in there somewhere but is too frightened to come out? I had thought that somehow he might just be . . . gone.'

Certainly, looking at Gamal, he did seem to be gone. Even physically he seemed to bear less resemblance to the boy we had known – he looked wizened and faintly yellow, and when he was not completely still, he had a nervous mannerism of twitching his fingers. Occasionally, a tear rolled down his cheek, which was all the more disturbing since he showed no other sign of feeling.

We sat in silence for a while, racking our brains for ideas to tempt Gamal.

'I think I know what to do,' said Finbar quietly. 'Music. That's what Gamal liked . . . likes . . . better than anything.'

I remembered then that Trewyn had owned a rough flute, and with a bit of a search we found it. For the rest of the afternoon Finbar and I took it in turns to pick out tunes on it. Did it make any difference to Gamal? It was hard to be sure. His hands moved more convulsively, and there were more tears than when we did not play, but there was no sign of the old Gamal returning. Late in the afternoon, when the pain in my leg was becoming so bad that I could no longer ignore it, I had a fleeting, shameful, longing to shake Gamal, as if to force him to talk to us.

Finbar, at my suggestion, had started dipping rags in cold water and spreading them over my badly swollen leg, alternating them with others as hot as I could bear. I began to shiver, and he put a hand on my forehead.

'You've got a fever,' he said gravely. As he helped me up the ladder to my bedchamber, I suddenly looked round the big room.

'Where's Moon?' I asked. The previous night Moon had slept on his beam, but I suddenly realized that I had not seen him all day. He had never stayed away during the day before. I began to weep hysterically.

'First the amulet, now Moon,' I said. I could not bear it.

Lying in bed, I could hear Finbar playing tunes to Gamal, and could picture the blank look on Gamal's face. I cried, as the pain grew worse and worse, and as I shivered and sweated with fever. Although we had got Gamal away from Meroot, I felt that I had failed in my *doran's* power. I had let the dog tear me, and the poison of the wound might easily kill me. Tossing and moaning, I knew that I had not wanted power with the 'purity of spirit' of which Euny had once spoken, but had wanted it in order to be superior to others. This reminded me of how hard it had been to relinquish the idea of inheriting my father's throne, of how jealous I had been of the unborn child who would supplant me. I had wanted the throne, as much as I had wanted to be a famous and successful *doran*. Now it was too late to be anything at all.

As the pain grew worse at times I seemed no longer to be in the white room, but to be back in the dreadful tunnel with the sound of snuffling and baying pursuing me. I would be conscious for a while of the bed and my pain, and then would be off once again down the dark, fearful corridors of my own mind. This torment went on, I believe, for hours. The house was quiet now – Finbar must be asleep.

Suddenly, I heard a baby cry. It was the cry of a very tiny child, a babe new-born, and it was as close as if it was in the room with me. I was so surprised that I sat up. The room shone with a blue-white light, and within it I saw the great throne in the council chamber, and my father in his kingly robes sitting upon it. What I saw was power – a certain sort of power – and it was attractive to me. It could be used well, I knew, not to gratify one's own vanity or to make oneself rich, but to make a country safe and prosperous, and to dispense justice. I had seen my father exercise his power in just this way. I knew I wanted it – I wanted the dignity, the respect, the sense of being the one to whom attention was paid, and to whom others had to listen. I wanted my father's throne.

Just then I heard the baby's cry again, weak but piercing. Its pathos moved me deeply. As I thought of it I could see the baby, a little naked boy child, wrinkling its face as it cried, feebly moving its tiny hands. I felt an unbearable longing to comfort and protect it, to use my grown-up strength and knowledge as a safeguard until the child grew big and strong. *This* was my rival, this frail, innocent thing? My mind moved unexpectedly away from the baby to Meroot. Meroot had wanted kingly power, had let her whole life be shaped into corruption by her jealousy of her younger brother. She had not noticed that her brother loved her, only that he had what she had not.

The questions and visions of the delirium boiled in my mind as if pushing me to some difficult, reluctant decision. Something had to be surrendered, or understood by me – I had to be different, but I did not know how to be different. Pain occupied the room. Sometimes I was wholly caught up in it, so that I could think of nothing else, sometimes it withdrew a little from me, and I was desperate to escape from it. What helped somewhat was the memory of Euny and her way of dealing with hunger; the pain would be worse if I fought it. I tried, not very successfully, to welcome it as if, instead of being a hated enemy, it was a favoured guest.

Was it part of the delirium or not? – at the time I couldn't decide whether I was dreaming – but I thought I heard Moon's wings sweeping round the room, and I felt the breeze of his flight cooling my hot forehead. Soon afterwards the pain became less, and I fell at last into a peaceful sleep.

It was morning when I awoke – a bright, sunny morning – and feeling weak after my fevered night, I lay motionless, conscious that the terrible pain had sunk to a mild throbbing. The

sun winked on something on the floor beside the
bed and I blinked, and then put out my hand,
disbelieving. For there, on the boards, with the
broken leather thong still attached to it, was the
silver amulet. Had it been caught in my clothes
and fallen out when I undressed? No, because I
would have found it the night before when I first
undressed. So how could . . .? Then the memory of
the sound of wings in the night came back to me,
and I looked around the room. Moon was sitting
comfortably on the beam, sound asleep. Only one
explanation seemed possible. Moon, my closest
ally, had gone back to find the amulet in the
tunnel and had brought it to me. I remembered
that it was after I heard the wings that the pain
began to subside and I fell asleep.

'I think you may have saved my life, Moon,'
I remarked shakily. And Moon, who usually
ignored my attempts to talk to him (a bit like
Euny), opened his huge amber eyes, regarded
me sternly for a moment, shuffled his feet a
little, and went back to sleep.

Chapter Twenty-Six

Gamal's Tune

'My mother has had a son,' I told Finbar.

'How on earth do you know that?'

'I saw it,' I said. 'In a kind of dream.' The swelling on my leg was gradually going down, and the pain subsiding. Finbar and I sat opposite one another at Angharad's hearth, with Gamal between us, as before.

'That will mean you won't become *regulus*,' Finbar said carefully.

'I know. I saw that, too. I think now that part of the reason I am a *doran* is so that I can protect the baby and the kingdom.'

'Don't you mind? It's unfair that you cannot rule because you are a girl.'

'It *is* unfair, and I did mind, very much,' I said truthfully. 'Now something has changed — I will use power in a different way.'

There was silence between us and we both looked at Gamal, wishing that my power might do something more for him. Finbar's patient work with the flute had had no effect on him at all. Suddenly I had an idea.

'The tune!' I said. 'There was a special tune, a rather beautiful lullaby, that Gamal remembered someone singing to him when he was a little boy. I think I know how it went.' Not stopping to pick out the notes on the flute I began to sing Gamal's tune to him, slowly, as I fumbled to recall it, my eyes fixed upon his face. When I had finished, not getting it quite right, I sang it again, this time remembering it completely. Now Finbar took up the tune, and the two of us sang it together, pouring into it our love and concern for Gamal. Then I noticed – or was I imagining it? – a flicker of interest in Gamal's blank face. It made me exclaim with surprise, but immediately it was gone, and I decided that next time it happened – if it did happen again – I should ignore it and carry on as if nothing had occurred.

Later that day, quite casually, Gamal put up a hand and touched his own hair. Finbar and I both pretended not to notice, but nothing more happened. That evening Gamal was as lost as ever.

'All the same,' Finbar argued, 'it does make you feel that someone's in there.'

Next morning Gamal coughed in such an ordinary, natural way that we both turned to him, expecting him to speak. As I fed him I felt I recognized for a moment a flicker of recognition in his eyes, though at once he stared in front of him again as if it was not safe to acknowledge me. Again and again we sang his childhood song to him, and again and again now, we felt sure that something was beginning to change inside him, though sometimes we felt we were imagining it.

'If he has come out of his hiding-place he needs to pretend he is still there,' I thought.

We were growing short of food now, and Finbar offered to go off on a foraging expedition, to try to buy meal and do some fishing. It was quiet in the house without him, and it was hard work washing and feeding Gamal all by myself. I busied myself cleaning Angharad's house – it would never do if she came home and found it dirty – and I kept the door bolted most of the time.

I was scrubbing the pots one morning when I heard Finbar calling me.

'Come and see what I've got, Juniper!'

I was so delighted that he had returned that I rushed to the door and unbolted it. Even as I swung the door open it came into my mind that Finbar always called me Ninnoc. There, just a few yards from the house, stood Meroot, holding her leather stick in her hand.

The two of us stood and looked at one another – aunt and niece, older woman and young girl, accomplished sorceress and raw *doran*. I trembled. How could I fight against her experience and her cruelty? Yet I knew too that I carried within me the good inheritance of all the *dorans* and that this gave me a special strength.

'What do you want?' I asked weakly.

'My son!' she said. 'I want Gamal.'

'You "ghosted" him,' I said boldly. 'You do not deserve to have him.'

'You are speaking of things you do not understand,' she said. 'I know you have him here and I have come to take him home.'

I was surprised to notice then that, although I was frightened of Meroot, I was much more frightened that Gamal would be taken by her and destroyed.

'You know that if a sorcerer steps on a *doran's* territory she is in the power of the other. I have power and I shall use it,' I told her, trying to keep the wobble out of my voice. For a moment she was transfixed by surprise at my apparent confidence. Then her voice rang out imperiously, 'I want my son.'

Just then, as the two of us stood and glared at one another, something totally unexpected happened. From inside the house came the sound of Gamal's lullaby, played with the hesitancy of someone who had not played the flute for a long time. Meroot was as startled as I was.

'What's that?' she said.

I had heard the melody many times before, played by Gamal on various instruments and hummed by Finbar and myself, yet it was as if I heard it for the first time, and was struck by its extraordinary power. It spoke to me of the simplest and best kind of magic, the magic of human love, the love of the woman who had taught Gamal the song, the love of Finbar and I who had longed so much to help our friend, the love I had begun to feel for the new-born little baby at Castle Dore, and the love of Gamal himself. Suddenly I saw the pathos of Meroot, with her desperate, scheming life, and her unreachable loneliness. She could have enjoyed the love of Gamal, and instead had nearly destroyed him.

To my surprise I found tears in my eyes when I looked at Meroot.

'It was hard for you when your brother took the throne instead of you,' I said softly. 'I am so sorry.' But Meroot would have none of my pity.

'And what will you do when *your* brother takes the throne instead of you?' she asked, taunting me.

'You know about that, do you?'

185

'If you return Gamal to me, I will help you get your father's throne.'

'Meroot, I am not a child, to listen to your silly promises. If my brother is the rightful king he shall reign at Castle Dore, and I shall do everything in my power to help him. As to Gamal, he shall choose for himself whether or not he returns with you, since you have forfeited your natural right to care for him.'

Amazed at my coolness I called to Gamal. Meroot seemed smaller, less dignified, than I remembered her. Suddenly Gamal, straight and tall, stood in the doorway beside me.

'I am not your son,' he said, 'and I shall not return with you.'

At this Meroot flinched as if he had struck her, but he went on.

'I have now remembered what I could not bear to remember – that when I was a small child you took me by force from the fair-haired woman who was my mother and pretended that I was your child. She was a *doran*, and a woman of great goodness, but you destroyed her. You had no child, but you thought you would use me to obtain King Mark's throne. You trained me as a soldier and you bullied and threatened me, to try to make me fit in with your schemes. Later you let the evil Knight work his spells on me. You thought it better he should torment me than that your plans should be frustrated. But now, thanks to my friends, I am free and I will never come back with you. I am no longer your son, Meroot.'

The look of mingled rage and pain on Meroot's face was a dreadful sight. She picked up her leather stick and threw it at me. One minute it was a stick but the next it had turned into a snake, and its head was within a few feet of me, its tongue flicking in and out of its mouth. Gamal and I stood as if turned to stone. I had neither my cloak nor clearwater to protect me, though I was wearing Euny's amulet. Now, I knew, was the moment of power, the shift in the balance of things between Meroot's magic and the kinder magic of the *dorans*. I bent and picked up the snake in my right hand and held it high above my head.

'The snake is now my snake,' I said, 'and it will do as I bid it. If you do not leave at once, without Gamal, and without troubling us any further, I shall order it to follow you wherever you may go, anywhere upon earth, and to bite you. If you leave now, without spells or tricks, you shall go with my blessing, Meroot. I am sorry for you, and I hope that one day you will be sorry for hurting Gamal. But now, the choice is yours.'

Meroot hesitated, her furious face fixed upon mine. Then unbelievably, she turned and, mumbling to herself and suddenly looking old and frightened, she shuffled away. I lowered my arm and gently let go of the snake, which almost at once turned back into the leather covered stick I remembered so well from her room at Castle Dore. For a moment I stood, trying to take in all that had just happened. Then, full of joy, I turned to embrace Gamal.

The two of us went back into Angharad's cottage and there – how could we believe our eyes? – were Angharad and Euny sitting by the hearth, as if they had been there all along.

'You took your time in despatching her,' said Euny, 'and you nearly spoiled everything with the flaw in the cloak.' But her face shone with pride in me. Angharad got up and hugged me with her old warmth. 'You did well,' she said.

There was feasting in Angharad's cottage that night – Finbar luckily returned in time to join us – and I think that I have never felt happier in my life. I loved sitting between the two *dorans* – I felt so beautifully *safe*. I looked across at Gamal. He was thin and pale, but life had returned to his face and his limbs, and he was again the boy I had ridden and climbed with so often.

Angharad remembered the fair-haired *doran* who had been his mother and answered many questions about her. Euny had visited my mother, had reassured her as to my whereabouts, and had seen the strong baby boy who was born on the night of my delirium. She insisted on looking at the scar on my leg, which bore an odd resemblance to a crescent moon. She touched the scar and murmured a spell over it, explaining that, like the flaw in my cloak, if I was not careful this could be a place where, in the future, dangerous magic might enter. I was lucky, I thought, in having such good allies as Euny and Angharad as I set out on my life as a *doran*.

'What will happen to me now?' I asked the two of them.

'It's for you to tell us,' said Angharad.

I considered.

'I want to go home first. I must see my brother and my parents. Then . . . well, they're not really going to need me, are they? I want to travel, to see strange places, to learn more . . .' I was thinking of the need to find the place I had seen in my dream, the house by the inland cliff. I had completely forgotten Meroot's plan that I should marry Gamal, but suddenly I wondered what Gamal would do and where he would go now that he had broken with Meroot.

'I am going to become a musician at last,' Gamal said, catching my eye. 'There is a monastery at Streaneshalch, far in the north, in Northumbria, where they are famous for their singing and for the tunes they compose. I shall go there and ask if I can learn from them.'

Finbar grinned. The quiet life of a monastery would not appeal to him.

'I could go back to being a page at your father's court,' he said, 'but really what I want to do is to go to sea. I'd like to become a great navigator, to discover new worlds and strange places. I shall travel to the coast and persuade a ship's captain to let me join his crew.'

Together the two boys and the three *dorans* lifted their wine cups to recall a famous saying of the *dorans*.

'To the mending of that which is broken,' said Euny, to which Angharad replied,

'And the finding of that which is lost.'

As the youngest *doran* present I said, 'It shall be so,' silently promising to do the work of the *dorans* as well as I knew how.

THE END

ABOUT THE AUTHOR

Monica Furlong has worked as a feature writer in Fleet Street and as a producer for the BBC. In 1978 she decided to concentrate on writing books, and she has become well-known for both her adult fiction and non-fiction titles. *Wise Child*, her first novel for a younger audience, was shortlisted for both the Carnegie Medal and the *Observer* Teenage Fiction Prize, and is already available in paperback from Corgi Books. *Juniper* is her second title to be published by Corgi Books.

WISE CHILD

BY MONICA FURLONG

Wise Child is frightened when she is sent to live
with Juniper, a young woman the superstitious
villagers fear as a witch. But she discovers no evil
in the magic that Juniper has to teach her – only a
desire to help others with herbal and healing skills,
and an understanding and awareness of the very
rhythms of life itself. Perhaps, Wise Child thinks,
she too could become as special a person as
Juniper.

But then her mother, the powerful sorceress
Maeve the Fair, claims Wise Child for her own,
tempting her with magic of a very different kind –
a magic to which Wise Child knows she should
never give in . . .

SBN 0 552 525979

A SELECTED LIST OF TITLES AVAILABLE
FROM CORGI BOOKS

THE PRICES SHOWN BELOW WERE CORRECT AT THE TIME OF GOING TO PRESS. HOWEVER TRANSWORLD PUBLISHERS RESERVE THE RIGHT TO SHOW NEW RETAIL PRICES ON COVERS WHICH MAY DIFFER FROM THOSE PREVIOUSLY ADVERTISED IN THE TEXT OR ELSEWHERE.

☐ 52617 7	**JOE AND THE GLADIATOR**	*Catherine Cookson*	£2.99
☐ 52525 1	**OUR JOHN WILLIE**	*Catherine Cookson*	£2.99
☐ 52645 2	**SO YOU WANT TO BE A WIZARD**	*Diane Duane*	£2.99
☐ 52646 0	**DEEP WIZARDRY**	*Diane Duane*	£2.99
☐ 52651 7	**HIGH WIZARDRY**	*Diane Duane*	£2.99
☐ 52597 9	**WISE CHILD**	*Monica Furlong*	£2.99
☐ 52595 2	**TRUCKERS**	*Terry Pratchett*	£2.99
☐ 52586 3	**DIGGERS**	*Terry Pratchett*	£2.99
☐ 52649 5	**WINGS**	*Terry Pratchett*	£2.99
☐ 52511 1	**ADAM'S COMMON**	*David Wiseman*	£1.99
☐ 52629 0	**BADGE OF HONOUR**	*David Wiseman*	£2.99

All Corgi Books are available at your bookshop or newsagent, or can be ordered from the following address:

Transworld Publishers Ltd, Cash Sales Department,
PO Box 11, Falmouth, Cornwall TR10 9EN

Please send a cheque or postal order (no currency) and allow £1.00 for postage and packing for one book, an additional 50p for a second book, and an additional 30p for each subsequent book ordered to a maximum charge of £3.00 if ordering seven or more books.

Overseas customers, including Eire, please allow £2.00 for postage and packing for the first book, an additional £1.00 for a second book, and an additional 50p for each subsequent title ordered.

Name: ....

Address: ....

....

We hope you enjoyed reading this book. If you would like to receive details of the latest new children's books published by Transworld Publishers, please send your name and address to: The Children's Books Editor, Transworld Publishers Ltd, 61-63 Uxbridge Road, Ealing, London W5 5SA, marking your envelope CHILDREN'S NEWSLETTER.